Redemption
ridge

Dorothy Yoder

Redemption
ridge

Dorothy Yoder

TATE PUBLISHING
AND **ENTERPRISES, LLC**

Published by Tate Publishing & Enterprises, LLC
127 E. Trade Center Terrace | Mustang, Oklahoma 73064 USA
1.888.361.9473 | www.tatepublishing.com

Tate Publishing is committed to excellence in the publishing industry. The company reflects the philosophy established by the founders, based on Psalm 68:11,
"The Lord gave the word and great was the company of those who published it."

Book design copyright © 2014 by Tate Publishing, LLC. All rights reserved.
Cover design by Junriel Boquecosa
Interior design by Jake Muelle

Published in the United States of America

ISBN: 978-1-63185-359-3
1. Fiction / Mystery & Detective / General
2. Fiction / General
14.07.08

For Glenn, Michael, and Janice
With love

There is a time for everything,
and a season for every activity under heaven:
a time to be born and a time to die,
a time to plant and a time to uproot,
a time to kill and a time to heal,
a time to tear down and a time to build,
a time to weep and a time to laugh,
a time to morn and a time to dance,
a time to scatter stones and a time to gather them,
a time to embrace and a time to refrain,
a time to search and a time to give up,
a time to keep and a time to throw away,
a time to tear and a time to mend,
a time to be silent and a time to speak,
a time to love and a time to hate,
a time for war and a time for peace.

—Ecclesiastes 3:1–8 (NIV)

ONE

Amber entered the sunporch to enjoy the beauty of the dawn. The rising sun unpeeled the darkness bit by bit to set the Westcliffe countryside aglow. The unfolding panoramic view of the Sangre de Cristo Mountain range mesmerized her. A strong draft prickled her skin and took her attention to the back door of the sunporch which stood ajar. Paralyzed by her vulnerability, she listened for any sound of movement within the cabin. Amber jiggled the deadbolt lock and inspected the doorframe—neither showed any sign of forced entry.

The cabin had been her temporary home for less than twenty-four hours, and Amber's emotional preference would have been to retreat into oblivion, but her analytical side rewound to last night. She had lounged in a chair on the sunporch and lost herself in an Agatha Christie mystery. She had journeyed through another time and place until the mantle clock had struck midnight, then had trudged to the loft bedroom. She had a vague memory of Brutus barking sometime during the night, but a specific memory of checking the lock on the back door eluded her.

Maybe I neglected to check it, she considered. That was a ridiculous notion. Her forte was managing all the little details of her career and her personal life. On the other hand, her recent layoff from a job that had captured her complete devotion, compounded by the blindsiding breakup with Todd, were still playing havoc with her wits. Self-doubt flooded in, and a game of torment began. Anything was possible.

The sharp retort of gunfire carried on the crisp mountain air like a clap of thunder. She jumped; her hand flying to her chest. The echoing gunshot had been so close it took a minute for her to convince herself that she was unhurt. Someone with anvils for fists pounded on the front door. Forgetting that she looked like a teenager at a sleepover clad in pajama bottoms, a T-shirt top and flip-flops, she made a dash to rescue the door from coming off its hinges.

"Keep that worthless bloodsucker off my property. If he goes after one of my calves, I'll kill him," the man said.

"Oh, I don't think Brutus would hurt a flea," Amber defended the dog that had been an unintentional part of the cabin rental.

"You irresponsible city folk come out here and think that you own the whole territory— that laws don't apply to you."

"Excuse me. I have never been called irresponsible in my life. You don't know me." She swallowed hard and motioned a shove at the gunslinging cowboy. "Take your nasty gun and vile attitude and leave."

"If I really wanted to shoot the no-good nuisance, I wouldn't have missed." The brazen man marched diagonally across the yard from the porch to the road.

Amber followed a short distance behind the man and kept him in her sights. She stopped when he turned into an adjacent property. Standing sullen and shivering in the middle of the road, she studied the landscape and had to admit that the gunslinger's ranch was impressive down to the split rail fencing enclosing the periphery. Moss rock columns supported a wrought iron arch with the words "Hunter Ranch" welded on it. The grand entrance heralded a log resort-like mansion nestled in the valley floor. Well-manicured shrubs and grass surrounded the building and flowed to a massive stone barn.

From her vantage point, Amber looked from one side of the road to the other. On one side, the Hunter Ranch was stunning. The county dump appeared to be on the other side. Pieces of rusted farm equipment were strewn everywhere, and vehicle parts littered the ground. A weathered, rough-hewn dwelling that appeared abandoned long ago was situated inside this metal dumping ground. Just beyond it stood a four-square-foot shack. A crescent moon carved above the door provided a clue that modern plumbing had never been installed.

Amber jumped at the sound of a high-pitched screech as the door of the privy opened in slow motion. Out stepped an elderly man whose form would have had to duck to clear the doorframe if his posture had been straight. He toddled along a worn path to the house, lingered in the doorway, and gestured as if he wanted to call to her. But no words formed, and he disappeared inside, leaving the door wide open.

These two properties take the meaning of opposite to a new level. They don't belong in the same county, yet alone across the road from each other. This gives new definitions to opulent and rustic. And what a poor old soul, Amber mused.

Red flags cropped up like wildflowers. First, Ilene and Max Grant, her landlords, had duped her into dog sitting Brutus for the summer. Then there was the sense that someone had been in the cabin with her during the night. And now, two very strange men were her immediate neighbors.

Amber had welcomed daybreak with the determination that this hiatus would alter the present direction of her life. But the contrary events of the day were far from encouraging, and her plan to live a few months in seclusion, already off track, left her no choice. She hurried to the cabin to call her best friend Olivia in Denver.

"Hi, Olivia. Don't fall off your chair. I know I gave you strict instructions not to contact me this summer, but I need your opinion on a couple of rather unusual incidents."

"Well, I'm somewhat disappointed, Amber. I thought you would last longer than a day as a recluse."

Amber was a little taken aback by the sarcasm. It was very unlike the Olivia she knew. She assured her friend that she intended to hide from the real world for the next few months, and there would be no more false starts.

"You wouldn't break your own commandment without a good reason. I'm all ears," Olivia said.

"I can't believe I came here for solitude and renewal. How can such a peaceful place be so dysfunctional? I should have followed my instincts. While I waited at the restaurant on Main Street for the Grants, I almost had a panic attack. Maybe this wasn't a good idea."

"You've never panicked in your life."

"You'd have to see it to believe it. When I pulled into the country store slash restaurant slash gas station, the only other movement on Main Street was a pickup truck going west and an eighteen-wheeler heading east. In passing, the drivers exchanged one short wave of their hands. I thought I had stepped into a movie scene. I stared out the restaurant window at the empty street. The Custer County school building holds the most prominent spot on Main. There was no amusement park, shopping mall, or a fast-food chain anywhere in the setting, not even a neon sign or traffic signal in the town."

"Well, that's good news. Traffic jams shouldn't be a problem."

Amber ignored the humor. "I felt cutoff from the rest of the world. I'm a city girl. I enjoy being spoiled by the convenient services and choices a large city has to offer. The fabric of my everyday life is woven with activities. Oh, Olivia, this world seemed minute when viewed through the restaurant window."

"Give yourself a break. You're accustomed to having people on all sides of you: traffic, pedestrians, and lines at the checkout counters. Even the sky here is full of jets, and people are on the move day and night. The lack of commotion will be eerie. It will take more than a few hours to adjust to. You said you wanted a change. Besides, you knew Westcliffe was a small town. What did you expect? Give it a chance."

"I know you're right, but somehow, everything here just seems wrong."

"This is what you wanted. You're not one to second-guess yourself. Don't start now. Well, you'll probably have to accept the fact that you have no control over most of this. Tell me about the Grants. Did they finally show up?"

"Yes, my panic-induced trance was broken by the excited chatter of Ilene Grant. She's pudgy and walked and talked at the same speed," Amber said. "Her hair was white with that blue hue, and she never stopped talking and smiling. In tow and equally short, but not chatty, was her husband Max, who appeared to accept his station in life. The lady riveted one sentence after another at the poor man. He only nodded occasionally. She said they had been delayed by a stop at the post office."

"So how does one get delayed at a small post office?" Olivia inquired.

"Vera, who works at the post office, would be my most reliable and knowledgeable source of information according to Ilene—gossip according to Max. I think that means Vera and Ilene are two of a kind when it comes to talking."

"I'm sure that wasn't an acceptable excuse to you."

"Right. Ilene really tried my patience. She did not show an inkling of thoughtfulness. Just spontaneity. But I'm glad they led the way to their cabin. Although it isn't hard to find, there was one confusing T-shaped intersection named Four Corners. That made me think."

Olivia laughed. "That does make you wonder what someone was thinking. Why name an intersection where three roads converge Four Corners?"

"It really makes me shake my head in disbelief. It's quite misleading. Maybe that's the point. But we finally reached the

Grants' cabin, which is positioned at a picturesque angle to the road and sits in a secluded meadow bordered by wooded areas of pine and aspen trees. The exterior of the cabin is covered in tan siding and trimmed in forest green, including the shutters and front door. A porch extends across the front, and the second story has two dormer windows. The final touch is a pair of forest-green wooden rocking chairs on the porch. They add a step back in time type charm."

"The setting sounds beautiful and just like the change you need."

"Yes, but get this. As I stepped out of my car, Ilene blabbed a dissertation about the Sangre de Cristo Mountains to the west, the Wet Mountains to the east, the Collegiate to the north, and Spanish Peaks to the south. And probably some in between that I can't remember. To me, they all start looking alike after a while. I give the pioneers a lot of credit for using them as landmarks. Anyway, I took one step and was hit in the back of my legs by a Saint Bernard. My knees just buckled."

"A dog?" Olivia asked.

"Yes, a dog. Get this. Ilene introduced me to Brutus, a huge dog. She said I'd like him. He's friendly, loves to go for walks, and is a good watchdog, a great companion. He wouldn't be any trouble and would require very little of me. Max finally injected one sentence into the conversation and assured me that Brutus is happy roaming the meadow, which is their property. Most of the neighbors around here still ranch their land, but the Grants' property is part of a ranch that was subdivided into forty-acre parcels. The Grants are the only lot owners to build so far. Anyway, Max said Brutus stays outside all the time and never wanders beyond the meadow. The dumb dog sniffed me, wagged his tail, and positioned his oversized torso so close to me that he knocked me to the ground. And then he licked my face."

Olivia chuckled.

"It's not funny, Olivia."

"I'm picturing it, Amber, and it is funny. You didn't mention dog sitting."

"That's the problem! There was no mention of a dog. I told the Grants that a dog was never part of the agreement. That I couldn't stay. Max said Brutus usually didn't warm up to strangers but had already taken a liking to me. They were almost on their knees begging me to stay. You know I'm not a dog lover. I've never taken care of animals before, but what could I do?"

"Couldn't they put him in a kennel? Olivia asked.

"I suggested that," Amber explained, "but they said he didn't like kennels. He is just too big to keep penned up. And they had this long story about friends in Colorado Springs who tried to take him before I arrived, but their yard was too small. He was just too big. The Grants kept insisting that he'd be no trouble. He's an outdoor dog. Would you believe the beast is more than two feet tall and about 170 pounds? His head is the size of a cow's, almost too big for his body. I can't believe I stayed. I was no match for fast-talking Ilene. They had a plane to catch. I hated to ruin their plans, and Max boasted that Brutus was good protection because his sheer size could frighten anyone or anything."

"Well, that should give you some comfort. You're alone in a remote area. I can't believe you aren't afraid."

"I was never afraid in the city. Why should I be afraid in the country? I'm used to being alone. That was my objective in coming here."

"You're right. There is no reason to be afraid," Olivia said. "Try it. If it doesn't work out, leave."

Amber hesitated. Something about the final turn of this conversation was odd. It didn't feel right. "Hmm, that'll be hard to do. The Grants went overseas, a last minute backpacking tour with some friends. They obviously have guts. Imagine roughing it at their age and in their shape. Anyway, contacting them will be nearly impossible. I'm embarrassing myself. I'm being a baby. I've handled a department of educated, innovative people. I should be able to handle a dumb dog."

Amber took advantage of Olivia's listening ear and rambled on about the old man and the would-be cowboy. After dwelling on these experiences, she made an abrupt goodbye. "I'm being silly. I need to settle down and tweak my attitude. None of this is that bad. I'm not giving myself enough time. I'll be fine. Sorry I bothered you with my tedious saga."

The next morning, Amber went for a walk along the road. Brutus was playful, getting in front of her and almost tripping her. "You ninny. Why do insist on cutting in front of me? You're ruining a lovely walk intended to improve my mood."

Brutus careened to the side of the road and sniffed some sagebrush. When Amber reached a crossroad, she checked over her shoulder. Brutus remained at the same spot with his nose now glued to a rodent hole. She advanced to a bend in the road. She commanded him to come. On the tenth call, Brutus gave up his snooping and looked her direction. At first, he lumbered his body in slow motion up the road and then took off like some kind of storm coming to her, ironically, with the excitement of a child chasing a puppy. When he reached Amber, he throttled down and was content to trot at her side. They walked on the road for several miles in surreal peacefulness. By the time they arrived back at the cabin, both were panting.

Amber prepared lunch and sat at the kitchen table. The cabin had all the conveniences of home. The main floor was one big open area. One wall of the living space was constructed of moss rock with a fireplace in the center. The other side of the room opened into a sunny kitchen with pots of violets in a flower window over the sink. The ambiance of the interior decor in shades of blue softened the glow of the contrasting green and gold terrain surrounding the homey abode. The furnishings were comfortable country with a splashing of antiques. The back of the piano displayed family portraits: snapshots of the Grants' past and present. The most charming and inspirational feature was a sunporch along the back of the cabin, which was enclosed in windows. No matter what the weather, Amber could sit on the porch and be surrounded by the natural world. A door exited off the sunporch to a deck and was the only back entrance to the cabin.

Amber's self-prescribed therapy for the season was twofold. Besides figuring out what came next for her professionally, she needed to overcome that sense of desperation and emptiness in the pit of her soul, the feeling that had been her constant companion since the minute Todd ended their long-term relationship. Over the last few years, she had longed for the luxury of time to read and explore. Since this summer was an unexpected gift of time, she planned to spend it in two ways. She would engage herself in a reading marathon and had brought along several boxes of books, best sellers and classics that she had collected—but had never found time to open. At the last minute, she had added to her stockpile a few self-help books that claimed they would unlock the doors to renewal and happiness. She also wanted to spend many hours hiking around the mountains, exploring the local landscape far from roadways. The objectives were complimentary to each other. She envisioned hiking for a while—finding a special spot and taking a break to read.

Before leaving Denver, Amber had driven to the mall and shopped for some mountain gear. She considered hiking boots, backpack, and water bottle necessary gear. She had walked past the guns, the skis, and the tents and found the hiking boots. After picking up and pondering a dozen pairs, she had selected a style that least resembled something a mountain man would have worn. The backpack section had been equally confusing with a variety of sizes and styles. Since climbing Mount Everest was missing from her agenda, she had chosen a feminine size in basic black. Selecting a water bottle had been easier.

The next morning, Amber placed *The Grapes of Wrath*, a water bottle, binoculars she used at the theatre, a light jacket, and a Granola bar in her pack. Squatting on the deck, she cinched up her boots and had enough shoelace left to hang a load of laundry. She stepped off the deck and called Brutus—who came rushing at her like a bowling ball.

Amber braced herself and scolded, "Settle down. You don't need to bowl me over. You're such a clumsy clod! Let's explore the Grants' property. You should know it well."

She tramped around, up and down inclines and through and around groves of ponderosa pines. In the meadows, the ground was heating up and radiated warmth around her. Amber, dressed in jeans and a sweatshirt, became hot. In the shade, she was comfortable, but sitting in the shade failed to inspire her. She quit after an hour and headed back to the cabin.

Brutus leaped around, trying to snag insects in his mighty jaws. "You look like a ballerina with both his legs in casts. How can the same dog be interested in chasing cattle one day and chasing insects the next? You're giving me mixed signals about your personality. You seem like a spontaneous, impetuous adolescent, but that rancher has a totally different opinion. He fails to see any redeeming qualities in you."

Brutus whizzed past her, circled around, and came up behind her and whizzed a second time. When Amber ignored him, he settled down, ambled up to her, and stayed on pace.

"I need to condition my legs to lift these lead weights on my feet. Each day, we'll go farther," Amber promised Brutus.

When they reached the deck, Amber sat on the step and took off her boots. With boots in hand, she stepped over the threshold of the sunporch and then took a step backward. She lost her grip on the boots, and they fell to the floor with a thud. An old man sat on one of the wicker chairs; his colorless eyes glued to the opposite wall.

Amber reprimanded herself when she was away from the cabin that she should lock it up. "What's your name? You live across the road, right?" she asked.

The man looked in her direction but did not answer.

"Do you come here often? Please tell me your name," Amber tried again. "Please tell me your name."

When he looked at Amber, she thought his eyes twinkled with recognition and fondness. The gaunt man scratched his head and seemed confused. Amber pitied the walking skeleton that seemed more defenseless than harmful. Perhaps food would elicit some meaningful response. "Are you hungry? Would you like a sandwich?"

A half smile was his answer.

As she made a chicken salad sandwich, Amber offered small talk about the weather and the beautiful valley. She'd pause now and then to give the old man a turn, but he did not utter a sound. Amber set the plate of chips, sandwich, and pickles on the coffee table in front of him. With dirt-crusted hands, he took the sandwich and gulped it in a few bites. When he had cleaned his plate, he leaned back in his chair. His eyes closed, and snores rattled deep in his throat.

"Oh, great. Now he's napping," Amber said to the walls.

Although her thoughts were scattered in every direction, she tried to read while he slept. In midsentence, her eyes drifted from the page of her novel to the shrunken hulk of a man. Both his plaid shirt and bib overalls were dotted with skillfully applied patches. She concluded someone had a skill lost a generation or so ago. The man's tired face still held a tinge of handsomeness.

Amber searched for answers: *Why is he there? Is he deranged? Why won't he talk? What should I do with him?*

Question after question popped into her head. After rereading the same page too many times, she slammed the book shut and studied the elderly gentleman. He looked frail and bony beyond anything she had ever seen, and she thought he must be on the verge of starving to death. Just before the sun fell out the bottom of the horizon, she heated some soup in a microwavable container and put it with some sliced French bread and two apples in a bag and returned to the sunporch. She wiggled his arm until he stirred. "Please wake up. You must go home while there's enough light out to see your way. I'll walk with you."

He arose from the chair. His legs remained planted until a delayed command to move started him in motion. They exited the back door, and Brutus accosted them. "Go away, you king-sized pest."

Brutus held his enormous head high and led the way. At a snail's pace, the man traveled from the deck, across the road and up the short distance to his front door. Amber had hoped to find someone at his house—someone who could answer some questions. When the old man opened the front door, the house looked darker inside than out. "Hello, hello, anyone home?" Amber yelled.

The old man shook his head and shot Amber a look like she should know better. She handed him the bag and instructed him to eat the soup while it was hot. She made her way back to the cabin in spite of the delinquent canine jumping on her and knocking her off track. She locked the porch door and checked it two more times before going to bed.

TWO

Numerous times over the next week, Amber found the old man wandering around the yard like a lost child. She fed him and talked to him each time she saw him. He muttered, now and then, words that were meaningless to Amber. Attempts to engage him in an exchange of viewpoints or get him talking about himself were either ignored or beyond his abilities. She was unsure whether he was a master of concealment or suffering from some form of senility. She concluded that he lived alone, and no one visited him. A rambunctious dog and a docile man, both insistent on shadowing her every move, sabotaged her plan to be a recluse. Something deeper than compassion prompted her tolerance toward the old man, especially on those days when she wrestled with the dilemma of sticking to her plan or her desire to make his life better. Slowly, she reconciled her perceived needs to his obvious needs. It presented a frustrating balancing act.

In midmorning, she found the old guy sitting in the hot sun on the deck. She brought him into the sunporch and served him a glass of ice tea. He relaxed there while she finished up some necessary household chores and made him a bacon sandwich.

After lunch, Amber walked him home. He shuffled into his house, shut the door, and left her standing on the road at his property line. Her gaze drifted from object to object in the incredulous yard.

"What a mess, Brutus. How is anyone ever going to clean this up?" Amber asked.

Brutus barked a reply and waited for a signal from her as to which direction they were going. She continued her observation. A building on the opposite side of the lane caught her attention. The windswept barn made one last stand against the climatic forces. The spine of the low-pitched roof was swaybacked, squashed by the weight of the winter snows. One half of the front of the building was open, and Amber could see stalls leaning every which way. Broken fencing surrounded that end of the makeshift barn. The other half was enclosed and had a door with rollers at the top that slid in a track. Roughly chipped holes in the boards beckoned her, as if they were spyglasses that could reveal the clues to a well-kept secret. Amber moseyed over to the shed and stood near a hole about her height. She put her hand to her forehead, leaning close to take a peek. Through the skiffs of light, she made out the form of a pickup truck, though details were indistinguishable. She stepped back, studied the door, and questioned her strength.

"Brutus, I assume that wisp of a man has opened this door. If he can do it, I can do it."

The metal track was rusty, as were the rollers. She put her fingers on the edge of the door and pulled. The door shrieked and moved a couple of inches. Amber inhaled a deep breath and tried again. The friction of metal on metal created the anticipated resistance. Amber strained until the opening allowed enough light for her to see the vehicle.

The tail end of the truck looked like her grandpa's 1952 Ford. The coincidence of seeing another like it catapulted her curiosity. She placed her body between the door and the frame and heaved until she could squeeze through. Once inside, she walked around and around the truck. It was a twin to her grandpa's in seafoam green and had a chrome grill with a Cheshire-cat grin. A nostalgic picture flashed through her mind. As a child, she and her brother had jumped up and down on the running boards in an effort to make the body of the truck rock. It had been one of their favorite pastimes when visiting their grandparents.

A twinge of homesickness for the good old days cascaded over her. She and her brother Trevor were only fourteen months apart in age and inseparable. Where she was, he was. Whatever he did, she did. During the preschool years, they were each other's world. Beginning in first grade and each year after, more distance spread between them as his interests centered on sports and hers on academics. Now, he was married with children and finding a common thread required effort. The breaking of bonds with special people had become a pattern in her life. Her strategic relocation to Westcliffe was calculated to end that cycle.

Amber circled the truck twice while assessing its condition. Although the tires had good tread and the body was solid, a paint job was overdue. Obviously, the classic specimen had been sheltered for the past few decades. The old man had enough wits about him to protect it from becoming another piece of vehicular art in his junkyard. Amber patted the fender on her way out.

The following day, Amber and Brutus trekked for miles behind the Grants' cabin. Amber sat in the middle of a meadow and read for several hours. In her viewing area, she and Brutus were the only two beings in the world. The thought provided some renewal. Brutus careened around her, entertaining himself through his sense of smell. A gentle breeze flirted with the ends of her auburn hair, and she closed her eyes to let the serenity soak through every pore. *Wonderful* was the only word that came to mind. She kept her eyes shut until Brutus decided to join her. She heard him panting and felt the warmth of his breath on her face. Before she had time to react, he knocked her over.

More amused than irritated, she said, "Brutus, you're a menace. You come out of nowhere, and you must learn that you're not a lapdog. I cannot hold you."

After a bit of a tussling with him, she managed to get to her feet. She brushed herself off and stretched her arms and legs. She gathered her belongings and leisurely hiked home. When the cabin came into view, she challenged Brutus, "Race you home."

Brutus won, and Amber went inside the cabin. She traded her boots for canvas slip-ons and popped the top of a cola from the refrigerator. She snuggled into a wicker sunporch chair, her hand automatically picked a self-help book off the end table. Relaxed and content, she read a few chapters and had just turned a page when the reverberation of gunfire pained her ears and shattered her concentration. Amber shot out of her chair and bolted to the front door. She opened it in time to see Brutus hightail it to the safety of the porch. "Get in here where I can keep on eye on you."

Brutus pushed his hulking body over the threshold and parked in front of the fireplace. "You're way too familiar with this room. I think the Grants have misled me on everything," Amber said. "What on earth am I to do with you? You give me no other choice."

Amber grabbed her car keys off the counter and lectured Brutus about destroying the place. "I hadn't planned to go into town yet, and I really regret that you are forcing me to. But I've got to get some answers and some kind of anchor for you. If you have one more encounter with that mean rancher, it will be your last. When I get back, I'll tie you up on a very short leash. It'd be in your best interest to stay out of trouble until I return. I would never hurt you, but I would put you in a kennel whether you like it or not."

At the Westcliffe post office, Amber checked the mailbox the Grants had opened for her. The possibility of having mail this soon was unlikely, but she went through the motions. To her surprise, what appeared to be a greeting card lay in the bottom of the box. Amber was miffed, but she took the card and stepped to the service counter in acknowledgment of the pair of eyes that watched her every move. She needed information, and if rumor had any truth to it, Vera should jump at the opportunity.

"Hi, I'm Amber Hanson. You must be Vera. The Grants told me you're an encyclopedia of Westcliffe facts and fiction. They recommended I come to you with any questions that I have about people or events. I'm sure you have a wealth of history stored in your head through all your experiences and acquaintances."

"I have worked in the Westcliffe post office for forty-five years. Yep, I started when I was a teenager. If my health cooperates, I'll stay on a few more years. I can't imagine anyone else doing my job. No one would know all the names in the valley like I do. I can direct mail correctly with as little as a first name, in some cases, even a nickname."

"Yes, I'm sure you'll be hard to replace."

Vera eyed the card in Amber's hand. "Looks like you have received an unusual card. I don't think I've ever seen such an artistic envelope before."

Amber's first impression of the small lady with the big reputation was undecided. Although Vera's permed gray hair formed a symmetrical bush around her circular head, thinning patches of hair revealed her scalp in places. Dressed in a denim jumper, she looked more like a civilian than a postmaster. Amber studied Vera who continued to talk.

"Now, Barb Sanders gets lots of letters from her family back home. She came from California after her very troubled marriage broke up. Janelle Moyer subscribes to every magazine published. If you ever want to borrow a magazine, she's the one to see—better selection than the library. If you want to stop by her place, I can give you directions. Old man Stoner is a recluse and hasn't received any mail in more than twenty years, doesn't even get junk mail. The rest of the world does not know he exists." Once started, Vera was mechanical. The words just poured out one after another. She became a radio, broadcasting on and on.

Amber listened and found some of the details interesting but tired of the rabbit trails. Everything reminded Vera of something else. Amber's head reached a saturation point, and her inner soul cried, *Stop!*

"I hate to interrupt, but I need to ask you a couple of questions. I had a rather unpleasant encounter with a neighbor. He's a man about fifty who lives in what could pass as a resort, and he packs a gun, rifle, or shotgun. I don't know some kind of firearm. He took some shots at Brutus."

"Not surprised. Not surprised at all. That would be Blake Hunter. He's as fiery as a volcano ready to erupt over any little thing."

"Sounds like a man fueled by determination, which would be admirable if there was an ounce of reasonableness to his behavior," Amber interjected.

Vera hesitated for a split second and frowned as if she didn't comprehend Amber's statement. "Yeah, whatever," she said, "his son BJ is just like him."

"He's married? What woman on earth would sentence herself to that? I pity his family."

"His wife died when BJ was little. That'd be about twenty-five years ago, and Blake turned all his attention to BJ. I think there was a lot of pressure on BJ to make his father happy. BJ was a good kid, maybe a bit arrogant, but popular. As big as that house is, I knew it wasn't big enough for the two of them. No one knows the particulars. There was some kind of falling out, which, of course, Blake has never talked about. BJ left Westcliffe a few years ago, and no one has heard from him since. Blake was miserable before, but now, he's beyond hope."

"How sad." Amber swallowed a lump in her throat. "Another broken father-son relationship. As time passes, they'll probably reach out to each other."

"I don't know. Both are as bullheaded as can be. I can't imagine either one backing down. Anyway, the Hunter family was one of the original settlers. They have always had the biggest ranch in the valley. Maybe Blake was different in his early years, but most of Westcliffe just knows him as a miserable son-of-a-gun. He's also the wealthiest guy in the valley. Most anonymous donations around town to folks in need and contributions to fundraisers are suspected to have come from him, but I don't believe it. Too bad, his disposition is so foul. He's really quite handsome."

Amber blinked in surprise. "Now, that I didn't notice. I was concentrating on the gun. Do you have any suggestions on how to approach a civil conversation with him?"

An elderly man shuffled to the counter. Amber stepped to a display of packaging materials and fingered the bubble wrap to fill the awkward minutes. She preferred that no one witness what could be perceived as prying into someone else's business. Vera conducted rather abrupt business and addressed Amber before the gentleman had slid his wallet back into the hip pocket of his jeans. "If you figure that out, let me know."

Amber got straight to the point and asked, "Where can I buy some rope? I think I need to keep Brutus tied up."

"Good luck keeping that mammoth tethered. He's strong as an ox, you know? That's odd. Ilene has never mentioned any problems with Blake." Without waiting for an answer, she continued. "Turn south at the liquor store. The hardware store is just down the road. You can't miss it, kind of sits there out in the open."

"Sounds easy enough. I have one other question. I'm also concerned about another neighbor: an old man living in a run-down house with an outhouse—"

"Old Joe," Vera cut her off. "That's Joe Stoner. The Stoners also were original settlers. I think Joe's about ninety-five, but no one knows for sure. He's lived here all his life. He was here before the rest of us and has always kept to himself. He chugs into town in his old pickup once or twice a year for supplies, mostly canned foods. I mentioned before that he hadn't gotten any mail for years." Vera took a breath. "I stand corrected. He gets one piece of mail each year—his property taxes. He always pays them, but I've no idea where he gets the money. Some people say there's some insanity in the family and that Joe has a touch as well."

"Doesn't he have any family, someone to look after him? He doesn't look like he should be alone, especially in such a primitive environment and all that litter around him." Amber asked, "Where did all those vehicle parts come from?"

"Joe's dad not only did some ranching, he was a self-taught miracle mechanic and could repair any kind of vehicle: tractor, truck, car. If it had a motor, he could fix it, but he never threw anything away, might come in handy as spare parts. Joe had a bunch of brothers and sisters, but one by one, they all died. Except for Joe. Joe lived with his parents all his life. They'd be dead twenty years now. They were a family of loners, kept to themselves, but there was something just not right about the whole brood. Joe's probably never been out of the county. I'd keep my distance. I've never heard anything good about the Stoners."

Amber's only thought was a question: *Why did I get caught between the two most mysterious people in Custer County, a madman, and a mad man?* She let the irony of her predicament disintegrate and responded, "Thank you. You have been very helpful."

She hastily left before Vera could start another subject and drove the few blocks to the hardware store.

A handful of male customers milled around. She sensed all eyes were on her. A clerk at the register directed her to the rope. After selecting the diameter and length she assumed appropriate, she hustled to the checkout counter. The same clerk chitchatted while he rang up her purchase. Amber made no effort to be congenial. She had her limit of small talk for the week. She waited for the automatic doors to open and felt the piercing stares of many eyes on her back. As she walked to her car with her shopping bag in hand, a gust of wind playfully sent dust devils swirling around the parking lot, blowing grit into her eyes. While protecting her eyes with one hand and juggling her purse and the shopping bag in the other, the bag fell to her feet.

"Here, let me help you with that, Miss Hanson," said a voice from out of nowhere.

Amber's eyelashes fluttered as she looked into a chest flashing a sheriff's badge. She bent her head upward to meet the gaze of a head bending downward and spoke without thinking, "You look more like a basketball player than a sheriff."

"I haven't played since college," responded the man as the wind tousled his brown hair, revealing streaks of golden sun-bleached strands. His bashful grin and blue eyes were unimposing, much too mellow for a lawman.

When Amber asked his name, more words come out than she intended: "You have an advantage. You know me, but you are? Perhaps the official welcoming committee?"

Amusement danced around the lawman's eyes as a short refrain of laughter was dispersed by the wind. "I'm Ryan Tanner, deputy sheriff. The Grants gave me a heads up that you were renting their cabin while they were traveling. I was driving by when I noticed the Jaguar in the parking lot. Can't say I ever saw one in Westcliffe before, especially at the hardware store. Thought I'd check it out."

"I don't really like driving it on dirt roads, but I'm only here for three months. Then it'll go back to Denver where I can pamper it, and so far, I've spent most of my time dog sitting," Amber corrected. She turned her back to the wind. "By the way, some guy named Hunter has taken a couple of shots at the Grants' dog. Is that legal? Can he do something that vicious? Claims Brutus will kill his cattle."

"He has a right to protect his livestock and his property. You should keep Brutus away from Blake's fortress."

"Rope in the bag. I don't know what else to do. He's not supposed to be in the cabin, but that's where I left him." Amber motioned to take the package from Ryan and noticed the span of his hand covered her purchase. She hesitated long enough to squelch the impulse of expressing the comment, which had already made its way to the tip of her tongue and instead, asked, "Have the Grants had trouble before?"

"Not that I know of, but most people settle these disputes themselves."

"I can't imagine having a civil conversation with Hunter. He's plain nasty."

"He lacks some social graces, you might say."

"I'd say he lacks personality."

Ryan tossed his head back and laughed. He reached into his breast pocket and handed her his business card. "Call me if you need help."

Efforts to sublimate her emotions failed as Amber drove to the cabin. Her interlude with Ryan amplified a forlorn feeling somewhere in her subconscious. She seldom felt lonely, and the strange sensation induced tears. She had yet to see any problem solved by crying, and shedding tears would not reinstate her job—the career that had been her life. Her mind shifted into automatic, and the scene of her dismissal rewound and played again. Every word, every movement etched in her memory.

Olivia had called the executives skunks, said it was a crime the way they use people, and had accused them of being a greedy bunch of "louses". That had not been Olivia's first choice of words. Olivia had advised Amber to confront Steven Kern, her former boss, and make him squirm with shame. To feel shame, he would need a conscience, and according to Olivia, that would require a transplant. Amber could count on Olivia to get riled up about most any perceived injustice.

Amber had insisted Steven Kern had no control over the decision. It was not his fault. It was a major downsizing. Profits had shrunk in the past couple years. Of course, the stock prices had followed suit. Payroll was always the starting point in shaving off big bucks from the budget. Amber understood the economics. Olivia had argued that Kern and other executives received bonuses of $18 million, or whatever the swinish figures were, during those same years. That was true, but they were all caught up in a culture of gluttony. It was mind-boggling. Amber choked and cleared her throat. She wished the whole nightmare would vanish.

Olivia was right. Upper management knew when to cash out their stock options just before a downturn. And all the execs' perks were protected. Complaining would do more harm than good. Amber's severance package was generous. She felt confident that Steven had negotiated the most lucrative deal he could for her. She refused to feel betrayed or entitled to more. Business was business. She had fed her own false security and disillusionment. She could find another job. The first and biggest disappointment was the realization that she was not indispensable. The second was the daunting amount of time and effort it would take to start over in establishing an occupational network, learning a new business, and all that stuff. After more than twelve years with one company, the dread of pounding the pavement overwhelmed her. She needed more time before tackling that mission.

High in the sky, the sun's penetrating rays beat down on her car. Amber opened her window and let the dry, warm air filter through her hair and evaporate the tears streaming down her porcelain cheeks. The scenic drive to the cabin seemed shorter than the trip into town. Some of the landmarks were becoming familiar, including the deceptive Four Corners. She parked in the driveway and stepped out of her car. As she shut the car door and turned toward the cabin, she was slammed against her vehicle by a huge furry force.

"Brutus, how did you get out of the cabin? You're impossible!" She manhandled her shopping bag as she navigated the obstacle course Brutus constructed each step of the way. Bounding at her side, he tramped on her feet and knocked her sideways; first one direction and then the other. She reached the safety of the front door, entered the cabin, and slammed the door in his face.

Amber plopped the package on the kitchen counter and with her one piece of mail in her hand, started toward the sunporch. As she entered, she tripped over her own feet when she saw Joe sprawled out on a wicker chair. He was staring at the mountains, lost in his own world.

"Joe, at least I can call you by name now. Please talk to me. I can't understand mumbles."

Amber knew better than to expect an answer. She prepared him a quick bagel with cream cheese and orange slices and left him eating while she went outside and tied Brutus to one of the front porch posts. The twenty feet of rope gave him more roaming room than she had originally planned, but punishing him for his lack of knowledge on property lines seemed unfair. "Mr. Congeniality, some watchdog you are. You let people walk right into the cabin."

Brutus wagged his tail and barked a proud "I know."

Amber cleared the dishes and joined Joe on the porch to read the card she had left on the coffee table. The envelope was decorated in a border of subtle geometric designs. The front of the card had the same designs. She read the handwritten note aloud.

> Dear Amber,
>
> Thank you for forcing me out of the company. It was the best thing that ever happened to me. I left an organization and boss who never appreciated me and got a great job that I love. My new job pays more and I actually like it. Thank you for doing me a favor.
>
> Grateful

She leaned back in her chair and let the note fall into her lap. After hitting dead end after dead end in her thought process, she spoke, "What's this all about? Who? Joe, who sent this to me?

The letter hasn't been forwarded. It has been addressed to my post office box in Westcliffe. I only gave that information to a few people. None of them would give it out without my permission. And from the tone of the note, I'm unsure as to whether the author is thankful or is trying to harass me. I can't say I appreciate either. I wish you'd talk to me."

Amber had fired very few people in her career, and after each firing, her boss had warned, "Watch your back."

None of the departures were recent. *Why would one of then send a card now?* She wondered. Finding a connection gnawed at her. Now was a good time to be out of the city and rid of a strange whistle that had followed her around Denver for months.

"This note is creepy and irritates me, Joe. The world keeps getting weirder," Amber said as she stuck the note in kitchen junk drawer.

That night, deep sleep eluded Amber. Brutus barked off and on. She listened for the sounds, which were many, as the cabin moaned and groaned as a weather front passed. Relentless thoughts of the people she had fired badgered her. Scene after scene replayed in her mind and stabbed at her heart, crushing her spirit. The first one to come to mind was Andy. She had hired him into a low-level position in the department and had asked him to leave before he had completed his probationary period. Based on his resume, his background was weak, and during the interview, he had trouble articulating his responses. The only reason she had hired him was because he was Laura's nephew. Laura was the head of another department and had asked Amber to give Andy a break. Laura took Amber to lunch and dominated the conversation, espousing Andy's merits. And she was relentless around the office. Against convictions based on logic, Amber yielded and welcomed him aboard.

Amber had found him likeable, and he showed genuine appreciation for the job. What caused him the most trouble was his lack of organizational abilities. In his position, he received a substantial amount of paperwork. By the end of his second week, his cubicle looked as if a bomb had exploded. Amber spent one Saturday helping him set up a filing system and giving him pointers on how to handle a piece of paper once. This was one of her most important strategies in managing an efficient team. She had delivered the advice enough to have the words engrained and on the tip of her tongue. "When a paper is in your hand, take care of it. Be done with it. Every time you pick it up, you are starting over with it. Revisiting its contents has an accumulative affect, and overtime bogs you down. Andy, you'll reach a point where you can't dig yourself out."

Andy had tried hard to keep up. He came in early and left late. He wanted to learn, but the skills he needed had to be intuitive. They were not in his makeup, and he had struggled every minute.

Amber had a department to run, which could only be as strong as the weakest link. Another piece of advice from Steven Kern came to mind: "Don't settle for a C student when A students are available." Amber agreed. Severing the relationship early was to everyone's advantage. She let the issue walk out the door with Andy and started looking for his replacement the next day. Neither she nor Laura had any further discussions about him.

In her opinion, sending a heartfelt thank you would be something that Andy would do. But not signing it would be uncharacteristic of him. And then there was Melanie. Melanie was a different story. Against Amber's strongest protest, Melanie had come into the department as a result of restructuring and had a villainous reputation as a backbiter. Amber had assessed Melanie's employment background and unearthed none of the necessary skills required to handle the job. Further evaluation disclosed a lack of work ethics. Yet Amber was saddled with a divisive problem employee with no redeeming qualities. No one had the guts to do the right thing by weeding out this tyrannical slacker. The unknown reach of her power and influence intimidated her coworkers and former bosses alike. At least once a day, Amber counseled Melanie about something. The reproofs vacillated between behavior and work performance. Amber was sure she could hear a sigh of relief around the whole company the day Melanie was fired. And Amber had lost no sleep over Melanie's self-inflicted plight.

Could the note have come from Warren? She wondered. She didn't fire him, but he always seemed irritated when she had tried to keep him on task. Ultimately, he left the company on his own.

As ceremonious as a changing of the guards, Amber watched the moonlight being replaced by sunlight. The earth was half lit when she slid out of bed and dressed in sweatpants and hooded sweatshirt. She descended the stairs and stepped onto the front porch. The trees, rocks, and mountains were silhouettes against the faint-blue heavens. *Thud!* Brutus's weight landed on the planks. Amber jumped and fell against the cabin.

"Good grief! Brutus, you scared me. I hope you slept better than I did. We'll do our walking after breakfast today. I'll need a nap this afternoon." Amber chattered to the dog as she filled his dishes with food and water. Brutus waited patiently for her to acknowledge him. Amber forced herself to stroke his short neck. His muscular build was hidden beneath a long brindle and furry white coat. His huge square head with drooping ears made him look sad, but his eyes twinkled with eagerness. Excitement overcame him, and he pranced, jumped off his front paws, and shook his head. His long tail swatted back and forth like a spastic pendulum, knocking a flowerpot off the porch.

"I can expect the unexpected when you're around," she lectured him as she set the pot back in place and replanted a geranium in what potting soil she could salvage from the ground.

Amber walked to the sunporch to witness the finale of the sunrise as her tea steeped. A breathtaking orange glow touched the mountain range and then gradually dispersed into hues of purple and blue before reaching a downy white cloud. The scene pulled her physically closer to the windows and mentally closer to the natural creations beyond. She stepped forward and bit her lip. The back porch door stood open again, creating a taunting, gaping way to the wilderness.

THREE

Amber sipped the last drop of her tea when the now-familiar reverberation of gunfire cut through the air. "Now what?" she demanded. Brutus was tied up as he had been for the last few days. She dashed to the front porch. Brutus's rope snaked down the steps. Its end lay unattended on the walkway with its fibers twisted every which way. Brutus scurried around the side of the cabin as Amber scanned the roadway in the direction of the Hunter ranch. Halfway between the Grants' and the Hunters' ranch, her eyes locked onto Blake's retreating broad back.

This has got to stop! He can't keep doing this. Amber ran after him. "Mr. Hunter, let's talk about Brutus," she yelled.

Blake Hunter kept his fast pace covering much roadway with his long strides. Amber turned up her speed and sprinted after him. When she was almost within arm's reach of the man, she shrieked, "Hey, you. I'm going to follow you until you talk to me."

As if strengthening himself for an attack, Blake froze in his tracks, and Amber slammed into his back with all her momentum, like a bird flying into a pane of glass. Blake took a step forward but stayed upright. Amber bounced off him and fell hard onto the packed road surface.

"You're as big a nuisance as that cussed dog. Go back to wherever you came from," he said.

Amber sucked for air as Blake looked on. When she could speak, she explained, "I tied Brutus up, but he chewed through the rope. I'm really trying here. Have you actually seen Brutus chasing your cattle?"

"You probably think it would be reasonable, even neighborly, to wait until I have a carcass? Then we could have lunch and exchange ideas about resolving the problem. You haven't a clue how the real world works, do you?" With that, he stormed away, leaving Amber on the ground.

There's no way I can keep an eye on that four-legged wanderer every minute. Amber steamed as she gingerly got to her feet and swatted at the dusty splotches on her pants. *And Blake Hunter is the most uncivil person on earth!* Fuming and winded, she returned to the cabin.

Although Brutus had created the drama, he lost interest when Amber began her chase of Blake Hunter. The dog crossed the road and commenced a sniff and search exercise in Joe's yard. Brutus nose poked with complete determination and focus.

Unaware of which direction Brutus had gone during her pursuit of Blake, Amber called his name every few steps, but Brutus did not respond. All she could see were squawking hawks circling toward the rear of the yard. Under any other circumstances, Amber would have savored the sight of the predators sailing on the thermal currents against the spotless blue sky. The mad cries sent an alarm to the alpine animal kingdom that also put Amber on notice.

Below the scavengers, Amber spotted the movement of Brutus's body among the clutter. The dog's head was hidden behind a vehicle hood propped against a boulder surrounded by piles of tires. His body was pulled taut against his four feet planted in the ground like pillars; his entire body drawn backward against an opposing weight that would not give.

Why me, Lord? I don't want to go tramping all over the country after this stupid dog. I don't want to see some dead animal. I'm sure the hawks have first dibs on it.

Dodging the litter as if she were crossing a minefield, Amber plodded across Joe's yard, calling the problem pooch with each carefully placed step. Brutus did not budge and continued his tugging, letting up, and then tugging again on something wedged behind the hood.

Amber tapped him on his back. "Brutus, come on. You're a bad dog this morning and are in big trouble. You'll be sorry if that's a skunk you're wrestling with." Her touch equated to a butterfly alighting on his back, not even sensed by him.

Working her hand along Brutus's side to his head, Amber made contact with his collar and clenched it. With all her strength, she pulled against the mighty dog's position. Exasperated, she took her eyes off Brutus, and let her gaze fall to the ground.

"Oh, dear God!" She closed her eyes and took a deep breath, praying to see something different on her second glance. But the pair of motionless feet protruding from behind the hood glared like Christmas lights back at her. These feet wore white leather sandals, not hiking boots or cowboy boots. Forgetting her own soreness, she pulled on Brutus's collar with a newfound determination. The dog let go of the body, and Amber pulled him home as fast as she could against his will. She applied her full strength until they both were inside the cabin. Her hands shook, and she was breathless as she dialed Ryan's number.

To bolster her attempt at regaining some composure, Amber went to the sunporch. If the room's ambiance failed, perhaps the mountain vista would carry her away. Both her feet lost contact with the floor, and she grabbed the back of a chair to restore her balance. "Jeez, Joe, you scared the life out of me. If you're going to keep showing up in my house, you must start talking to me. You've got a big problem right now."

While the sheriff and deputy sheriff inspected Joe's yard, called the coroner, and began their investigation, Amber paced the porch floor. Joe stared into space, and Brutus stretched out in front of the fireplace.

"Any minute now, the Westcliffe posse will be knocking on the door and have a bunch of questions for us. You two know more than I do, but I'm the one who is going to get grilled. What did I ever do to deserve the two of you? You're going to drive me crazy!" Amber wanted the dog and the man to know how displeased she was with both of them.

After waiting for what seemed like forever, the expected knock on the front door, nevertheless, startled Amber. She opened the door and found Ryan and the sheriff both standing at attention. The sheriff introduced himself as Gavin Rivers. His taupe-colored uniform was brought to life by accents of Western wear from his Stetson hat to a silver belt buckle the size of a platter and to his polished boots. The outfit was complete and dapper. Amber invited them into the sunporch and offered them a seat. Both declined and remained standing, as did Amber.

"Amber, we would like to ask you a few questions," Gavin began.

The first name basis threw her for a minute. Sheriff River's formal posture misled her into anticipating "Ma'am" or "Miss Hanson."

Although Gavin never removed his sunglasses or hat, a tanned face and chocolate-brown hair were evident. Amber guessed him to be about her age and suspected daily workouts were a priority. He was polite and professional and much to her surprise, thoughtful and friendly.

Gavin conducted the official questioning. "Amber, have you heard anything, seen anything, seen any cars loitering in the area? Have you heard or seen anything out of the ordinary?"

Amber wanted to scream, "Ordinary? Are you kidding? Nothing I have encountered has had any resemblance of ordinary." Instead, she politely answered a simple no to each question.

Gavin concluded with a statement to the effect that he would not ask her to identify the body, because the birds and other critters had been ripping on the flesh. All they knew was the body was a female and did not appear to be anyone they recognized.

Both lawmen asked Joe questions and tried to engage him in conversation, but he remained his usual mute self and stared straight ahead. A herd of wild horses could have stampeded through the house without a flinch from Joe.

Gavin advised, "Amber, with so many unanswered questions, maybe you shouldn't have Joe in the house."

"You can't possibly think Joe had anything to do with this. Joe doesn't have the strength to swat a fly. He may be out of it, but he has a sweet disposition. He hasn't shown any violent tendencies." Amber stopped herself from telling the lawmen that she had no way of keeping Joe out of the house. He entered without invitation. "Maybe you should talk to Blake Hunter. There's a man who seems capable of most anything, hell-bent on protecting his rights, no matter how unreasonable that might be. He should be your first suspect."

Amber caught the officers exchanging glances and wished she had kept quiet. The less she said, the better. She clammed up before any more foolish remarks or accusations were uttered. Ryan took Joe by the arm and escorted him out the sunporch door. Gavin excused himself and exited the same way.

For the rest of the day, Amber kept Brutus by her side. They took a time-out from hiking and holed up in the house. Joe returned in late afternoon. Amber fried bacon, eggs, and potatoes for him.

"I know it's not breakfast time, Joe, but I don't feel like cooking, and I can't stomach food myself right now."

Amber wanted nothing more than for everyone to leave her alone and was relieved when Joe scarfed down his meal and left. She cleaned up the kitchen and saved the bacon grease to pour over Brutus's food in the morning, not that he deserved any special treat. Her final thought before falling asleep on the sofa was that morning could not come soon enough.

Amber opened her eyes to bright sunlight pouring through the windows. She squinted at the mantel clock and sprang off the sofa, giving Brutus a start.

"It's almost nine o'clock, Brutus. How did I sleep so late?" She dashed to the sunporch for her habit forming morning gaze at nature and exhaled a long breath at the sight of the open door. "I give up," she declared. She dressed with a new nervousness and urgency and drove her Jaguar down the gravel roads faster than necessary. Her trail of brown dust lingered long after her passage. At an intersection with a paved road into Westcliffe, she rolled through the stop sign. Her eyes were on the road, not on the speedometer or rearview mirror. At the startling short blurt of a siren, she glanced in the mirror. Sure enough, the flashing lights were for her. "He came out of nowhere," she said aloud. She braked hard and pulled to a stop on the shoulder of the road. Her mind whirled in pursuit of a defense. She had no idea what the speed limit was, or how fast she was going. She said a quick prayer that the officer would be Ryan. She rolled down her window and took a deep breath at the sight of the unforgettable silver buckle.

"In a hurry?" Gavin asked.

"Yes. I need chain to secure Brutus, the St. Bernard, so he can't chase the neighbor's, Mr. Hunter, cattle, and I overslept, and I have a lot of things on my mind." Amber stopped talking and realized how unimportant and minimal it all sounded. "I'm sorry, Sheriff Rivers, my mind was somewhere else. I know that there is no good excuse."

"Well, let's start with the basics. Could I see your license and registration?" he asked.

Amber fumbled in her purse and glove box and produced the documents. She had never been issued a ticket and resented how it made her feel like a child.

Gavin looked over the information and handed the papers back to Amber. "Watch your speed," he warned. "You're not on a racetrack."

Amber opened her mouth to say thank you. Before the words were spoken, he added, "Have a nice day." He returned to his cruiser, did a U-turn, and drove off in the opposite direction.

At the hardware store, she bought a chain. She drove to the post office, checked her post office box, and found another card. Amber squared her shoulders, determined to appear calm, to act like everything was fine, that *she* was fine, and she went to Vera.

"Vera, does Joe have a speech problem?"

"Heavens, no. He can talk when he wants to. Tight-lipped like his old man, that's all. So you met Ryan at the hardware store. What a good-looking young man. He's the local heartthrob."

"*How on earth do you know that?*" Amber refrained from blurting. That meeting now seemed like eons ago. Amber was repulsed by the fact that one person or another knew her every move. She staved off the impulse to give Vera a stern lecture, but in reality, Amber knew no good would come of that. Vera was Vera. She decided to stay on Vera's good side and played along instead. "Oh, unmarried?"

"Divorced and somewhat eligible. Jessica and Ryan dated all through high school. They were inseparable. They both went to Gunnison to college and married after their first year, divorced right after graduation. It was a real shock. She moved to Boulder and went into real estate. She wanted more than Westcliffe. He didn't," Vera said.

"Who wouldn't?" Amber felt like a wooden dummy propped on someone's knee as the words tumbled out of her mouth in a voice that was strange to her own ears.

"What? Speak up. I missed what you said."

"I'm sorry. I was saying, 'Who could've seen that coming?' How sad for both of them."

"I think they both are quite happy now. They've moved on. Now, he's seeing Meredith. She's a divorcee with two daughters and teaches third grade. She came here for the job but isn't cut from the right cloth to be part of this community."

"How's that?" Amber asked, but she was uncertain why. Fascination with either small town gossip—or Ryan's personal life—stretched her imagination beyond its limits.

"Meredith and those girls drive into Pueblo or Colorado Springs several times a week just to shop. Shop, shop, shop. That's all they ever do. That's way too superficial for Ryan. Change of subjects, but you sure had some excitement at your place."

Amber replied, "More like trauma, and it actually was at Joe's."

"Yes, I know it was at Joe's. But you're almost right across the road. It just seems to have more to do with you than with Joe."

"What do you mean?"

"That's just how I see it. Too many strange things happening out there since you came."

Amber did feel like the oddball in town but resented being blamed for the oddities of her environment. She squelched another lecture and composed herself. "Anyway, news sure travels fast. I sure hope they can identify the body quickly. That would help settle the old nerves."

"Well, there is no such thing as crime-scene investigators here. That'll come from Colorado Springs. It will take some time." Vera said and eyed Amber, "I hear she was a city person like you. Perhaps you knew her."

Amber had had enough for one day and enough conversation about the dead body. Her mood was heading south and prompted her to make an abrupt exit.

As she rushed down the post office sidewalk, Amber came face-to-face with Ryan. "I forgot to mention that Blake Hunter's still using Brutus for target practice," she said and stormed to her Jag and spun off. An inner voice nudged her to head in the direction of Denver—to run as fast as she could away from all the problems that continued to pop up. Her self-disciplined character overpowered her feelings and forced her to honor her obligations. She turned in the direction of the cabin and obeyed all driving regulations.

Amber parked in front of the cabin and had almost walked to the porch steps before she noticed Joe at the far end propped against the porch post. She unlocked the door and let Brutus out. He jumped on her, as if trying to land in her arms and barked. His inability to contain his excitement tickled her, and she gave him a hug to settle him down. In a weak moment, she had also bought a rawhide bone for Brutus to chew on. She presented it to him, and he flopped down in place to gnaw on it.

"Decided not to let yourself in the back door this morning, Joe?"

"I've been waiting for you. I need to talk to you. Something terrible has happened. I don't know what to do." His head hung to his chest, and his hands hid his teary eyes. The sight confused Amber. She was thrilled that Joe not only was talking—he was making complete sentences and displaying emotion.

Amber sat down beside Joe and put her arm around his frail shoulders. "Tell me. Tell me what has you so upset."

"I can't find Sarah. I must find Sarah." He got up, paced the length of the front porch. Amber paced with him and quizzed him about Sarah.

"Joe, are you hungry? Come inside, and I'll make lunch," Amber coaxed.

"No, no, I must find Sarah," Joe repeated.

Amber's mind raced. *Who is Sarah and why is he so agitated about her?* Food was the only tranquilizer she had to offer.

"I'll be right back." Amber slipped into the cabin and took two Granola bars from the cupboard and two apples and bottles of water from the refrigerator. She returned to the front porch where Joe had taken a seat in one of the rockers. She handed him an apple and unwrapped the granola bar for him. She sat in the other rocker, and they nibbled in silence.

When Joe had finished, he stood and began to pace again. Amber convinced him to take a couple sips of water. He leaned against a porch post and looked toward his house.

"Sarah, I must find Sarah," he said as he took off like a jackrabbit and almost fell as he stepped off the porch.

Joe crossed the road. Amber and Brutus followed as he trekked past his house and outhouse and continued at a steady clip. A fair-sized shed stood beside a stand of ponderosa pines about where the field of vehicle parts ended.

Amber stopped. "Joe, what's this building?"

Joe was yards away, head down, and rocketing onward. Amber sped up to catch him and repeated her question and then let the question die for the time being. She would try again when they returned from wherever it was Joe was heading. It made sense to Amber that Joe's dad would need a workshop. The discovery piqued her curiosity. If the inside were in the same shape as the parts yard outside, it would be such a mess she had trouble envisioning any free space in which to work.

Amber felt faint at the possibility of the dead body being someone named Sarah. Her knees became even weaker at the thought that Joe might know the dead women. She slowed and mulled over the notion. *Maybe I have overlooked some danger signs. If I searched, how many other bodies might I uncover among vehicle parts?* Joe's lifestyle could hardly be called normal. Brutus came to her side and nuzzled his nose against her hand. "I would like to think that you'd protect me, but I know better. Should I be afraid of Joe? Should we turn around and go home?"

Brutus pushed at her hand in an attempt to get her to pet him. Amber leaned down and stroked him. "Ridiculous, Brutus. I'm being ridiculous. I could knock Joe over by blowing on him. Let's catch up to him."

They jogged to Joe and walked up a slight incline and weaved their way through a heavily forested area that led to a clearing lit only by slight sunlight through the thick trees. The sound of the summer breeze hummed as it filtered through the boughs, and the damp smell of pine lingered like a heavy mist. Pinecones crunched beneath her every step, agitating the birds hidden in the thickness of the pines. In the center of the clearing, eleven wooden crosses stood in a zigzag row. Two of the crosses had tumbled face down on their respective graves. Withered by time, they rested among the grasses, and Amber assumed they had been there the longest. One cross was painted white with the name Sarah written in perfect penmanship. The names on the other weathered crosses were hard to decipher. Amber studied each one until she could make out the names. Only a first name and an age were listed on each cross. Luke was written on one cross without an age, and Mary on another also was ageless. Amber concluded they were the graves of Joe's mother and father. All the others had died at various ages in childhood.

"Joe, did your brothers and sisters die in a plague? Did they all get sick?"

"No," Joe answered with clarity.

"How did they die?"

"I don't know. They'd be here one day, and the next day, they'd be in one of these graves."

Amber rubbed her arms to generate some heat. Her entire body was in the grip of a chill. "Did your parents hurt them?"

"No," said Joe. As blankness began to creep over his face, he asked again, "Where's Sarah. Where's my Sarah?"

"Is this your Sarah? I think she died, Joe, probably a long time ago. The grave marker says she was nineteen. She lived longer than any of your other brothers or sisters." *Keep him talking. Keep him talking.* Amber chanted to herself.

"Sarah is my favorite person in all the world. I love her. She always protected me and took care of me."

"Protected you from what? What happened to your brothers and sisters?" Amber asked again. "Did your parents hurt them?"

"No, I don't think so. I don't know." Joe's breathing became rapid, and he paced back and forth in short steps, as if movement could sooth his anxiety.

"Joe, please relax. Everything's okay. Let's just talk about what you remember. If your parents didn't hurt your brothers and sisters, did someone else?"

"Well, it seems like, or I kind of remember, that sometimes, they wouldn't let them eat. Sometimes, they made them stay outside on the step."

"You mean your parents? Did they punish you like that also?"

"I don't know," Joe whispered. "I don't remember."

"Joe, I don't believe you can't remember. If you tell me, I can help you. I need to understand before I can make things better for you. Please think hard. Try to remember. Did your parents punish you like that?"

"Yeah." Joe's reply was immediate. "But Sarah would sneak food to me and take the blame for me. I miss my Sarah. I think she had to leave, but she'll be back."

"Joe, did you go to school?"

"No, my mother taught all of us kids. She was smart and had lots of books. I still have all of her books. My dad never wanted any of us to go into Westcliffe—said it was full of sinful people. That we'd be better off not sitting next to them in school, or walking down the street with them in town, or singing with them in church. That's what he always said."

"That is beautiful handwriting on Sarah's cross and your parents' crosses. Is it your writing?"

Joe nodded his head and fought back tears.

"Would you show me your books, Joe?"

Getting inside Joe's house was a cinch compared to getting inside his head. In a gait faster than an old body should move, Joe took off for his cabin with Amber and Brutus on his heels. As they approached the shed Amber touched Joe on the elbow and asked him about it. Joe stopped, looked straight ahead, and stared into space. His face had lost all color.

"Joe, are you all right? Can we look in the shed? Maybe you can sit down and rest."

"No, no, don't go there. No, no, awful place."

"Okay, okay, Joe. That's fine. We won't go there," Amber soothed. "I'm really excited about seeing your books. Let's go."

Joe resumed his pace and starting talking about the books before they reached the front door. Joe explained as he entered the main room, "I've moved all Ma's stuff into this back room." Amber dawdled in the main room, trying to notice as many details as possible. She had anticipated the worn, bare wooden floor but was shocked by an upholstered sofa and matching chair. In some spots, the fabric shone, and in others, stuffing poked through. Both sagged in their middles. The sofa was flanked by two unmatched end tables with kerosene lamps on them. The kitchen area consisted of a wood-burning cookstove, crudely made cupboards and shelves, and a long handmade table with wooden benches shoved against the wall. At the other end of the room, Amber could see bunk beds in the long lean-to addition.

Amber stepped into what she would classify a cubbyhole. On one wall, orange crates were stacked from floor to ceiling with books squeezed in every inch. A small desk pushed into the corner was covered with workbooks and papers, including tablets and paper ruled for practicing the Palmer Method penmanship. In an almost alarming childlike demeanor, Joe showed Amber his workbooks. His handwriting was flawless, and algebra problems were done correctly.

"Where did you get all these books?"

"Ma was a school teacher when she was young. She read all these books over and over again." Joe's eyes looked beyond the walls of the room. "Sometimes, she'd scream that she wanted new books to read. Then she'd cry for days and not talk to any of us."

"Why didn't your mother go to town and buy a new book now and then?"

"When all the kids were little, Ma never went to town. She had to take care of us, and Pa said there was no need. He could get everything we needed."

"Wouldn't your father bring her one?"

"I remember her asking him to, but he'd come home without one. Always said he'd run out of money. She finally stopped asking. As she got older, she lost interest in books anyway. She had really bad headaches and stayed in her room alone—sometimes for days."

"That's so sad. Your mother must have felt powerless."

"Sometimes, there would be a new book, and Ma would be so happy for a while. I never could figure out where the books came from."

Amber was determined to keep him talking. "Have you read any of these books?"

Joe's facial expression went from dull to bright as he pointed to one book after another, giving Amber a brief summary of the contents of each.

"I believe you have read all these books."

"Yeah, a few times."

They stepped back into the main room where Amber noticed another doorway. A ragged cloth shirred on a rod hung inside the doorframe of another room. *That would be Joe's bedroom. Even if most were children, how on earth could so many bodies live in such tight quarters day after day?* The thought was depressing, and Amber fought the urge to bolt. Anyone who lived like this would have a touch of insanity from being bored, from literally stepping on each other's toes, and from lack of contact with the outside world.

The walls closed in on her. An hour in this closet of a house was more than she could handle. She turned to say good-bye.

Her eyes met Joe's, and he smiled a broad grin that erased ten years from his face.

"I'm so glad you're back, Sarah."

No, Joe, I'm Amber not Sarah. Sarah's dead. The words formed in her mind but never made to her lips. The happiness and peace on Joe's face overwhelmed her senses and steered her in a different direction from her instincts. She left without saying a word.

Amber walked home and sat on the front porch, stroking Brutus. All she could think about was the contrast between the condo she called home and what Joe had lived in.

Her condo was located in a historic warehouse building in Denver's lower downtown district called LoDo. It and other run-down buildings in the area had been renovated into lofts, condos, commercial buildings, and retail shops. LoDo was touted as one of the most in vogue and expensive parts of Denver. The setting was worth all the long hours she had spent at work. The most rewarding part of every day had been coming home to the charm and warmth of the old redbrick building on the tree-lined street.

Amber recalled lounging on her west-facing balcony to savor the unobstructed view of the Rocky Mountains: serene, peaceful, and nature at its grandest. To the northeast, the Mile High City spread out at her feet: noisy, busy, and exciting. Inside her refuge, the trendy living area was decorated in rich colorful tapestries purchased from upscale interior design studios and in soothing artwork bought from galleries around Larimer Square and the greater downtown area. She could almost feel her fingers glide over a marble statue of Aphrodite. The graceful Greek goddess of love and beauty assumed a prominent position on the mantel. The smooth white stone of the sculpture against the rustic redbrick fireplace created a focal point that could be seen from many vantage points in the condo. The most premier designers could not have found anything more perfect for the ambiance of the room.

After one problematic year-end close of the financials, Steven Kern, her once esteemed boss—now a traitor from whose actions she was trying to overcome—had surprised her with the statue. He had called her into his office and presented it to her.

"Amber, I bought this especially for you. When I saw it, I thought of you. This is from me, not the company. Please don't tell anyone. This is just between you and me. I really appreciate the effort you have put into building a good team. It's my way of saying I see what you have accomplished and know how much work it took to get there. I wanted to do something special and personal for you."

If she were at her condo now, Amber would push the sound system on button and curl up in her favorite wingback chair to be lost in the melodies of "Adagio" by Karajan. But she was not there where everything had been safe and orderly. She was in Westcliffe where everything seemed to be in a tangled mess.

Crickets creaked a soothing song, but she did not hear. The cool night breeze raised goose bumps on her arms, but she did not feel. Her stomach whined and groaned, but hunger did not set her in motion.

Sometime during the darkest part of the night, she stumbled inside with Brutus. She lit a fire in the fireplace and curled up on the floor using Brutus as her pillow. The day had shaken her, and her thoughts spiraled: *Is life one big lie? Is happiness real? Why are there problems everywhere I go? Why is this train wreck happening to me?*

FOUR

mber awoke in a zombie state—her body stiff from sleeping on the floor, and her mind in idle. Brutus, full of energy, jumped around the cabin, barking at her and insisting she play with him. She opted for a less ambitious run with Brutus. They went outside and headed down the road. Brutus took the lead with vigor and made Amber run to keep up. The bright sunlight launched a piercing pain in her head, and the air, still cool from the night, gave her a sudden chill. Amber slowed to a stop, leaned forward, and put her hands on her knees as she gasped for air. She called Brutus to her: "Sorry, Buddy, a short jog is all I have in me this morning. I forgot my sunglasses, and I need some caffeine to jumpstart my systems."

Amber slowed her pace to a fast walk, while Brutus trotted beside her back to the cabin. She fed and watered him and threw her arms around his neck in a big hug before securing him to the new chain. "Unless you have a hacksaw hidden around here, you won't be escaping now," she advised him.

She brewed strong coffee and stared at yesterday's unopened card. In one decisive motion, she grabbed it from the kitchen counter, tossed it into the wastebasket, and gave herself a mental pat on the back for taking command over something, even if it was an inanimate object. With coffee mug in hand, she plopped herself down in a wicker chair, picked up her book, and read.

In the afternoon, she and Brutus walked the property behind the Grants' cabin. "Okay, Brutus, here's the plan. Today, we are going in a different direction for an hour or so. Let's see if we can discover some points of interest."

Other than finding stakes in the ground with lot numbers on them, the landscape changed only slightly from lot to lot, offering nothing noteworthy or compelling. Each parcel had hills and valleys, pine trees, wildflowers, and views of the Sangre de Cristo Mountains and other ranges. From a distance, their steel-gray color against a crystal-blue canvas dramatized their strength. She felt in the presence of something huge, powerful and wondrous, of a beauty beyond her vocabulary. The picture inspired awe. She felt a rapport between her inner self and the spirit of the natural world surrounding her. The peace delivered by the scene satisfied her longings on the surface, but she could not sustain atonement of the deeper desires of her heart. She could not articulate what she was searching for, but she would know it when she saw it. Disappointed, Amber returned to the cabin in late afternoon.

The next few days, Amber's schedule became routine. She and Brutus hiked the area behind the Grants' cabin in every direction, except in the direction of the Hunters' ranch. Since the properties were adjacent, she declined to step foot on any soil that might belong to Blake. She found the possibility of getting shot at or chased by a bull two powerful deterrents.

She paralleled the property line marked by weathered fence posts that separated the rough native area from a field of young hay. On the other side of the hay field, a lush emerald pasture had been nourished by spring runoff from the high country. This natural irrigation system had made ranching in the valleys possible. A herd of Black Angus cattle mowed the grass to the right height, leisurely grazing the meadow everyday. Amber heard the faint bellow of a cow for her calf. Once emitted, the call was repeated many times among the herd of mommies and babies.

The landscape failed to beckon her or entice her to linger at length. Amber and Brutus roamed and searched for the right spot to stop and read. The area held its own beauty but in a typical or ordinary way. Amber had set the bar high. She wanted special—something that moved her beyond imagination and description.

Returning to the cabin after their last exploration, Amber admitted defeat. "That's it, Brutus. It's probably me. My mood is in a funk, but we're done on this side of the road. I find no appeal here. Let's go call Olivia and give her an update."

"Hi, Olivia. You sound out of breath. Did I catch you at a bad time?"

"Oh, I just came home from working out at the YMCA. With my big frame, if I let up on the exercise, I would look like Paul Bunyan. You, fortunately, can eat everything in sight and not gain an ounce."

Amber laughed. "You do exaggerate. But seriously, I need you to help me sort things out. I can't believe I'm calling so soon again, but I need a sounding board. My simple, quiet retreat gets more complicated everyday. I thought the innate beauty here would renew my soul, but so far, it has done nothing but unravel my nerves. I have no control over anything! Everything is so thorny! I don't even know where to start."

"You sound serious. Is everything okay?"

Amber replayed the events around Brutus and shared details of the latest encounter with the mad-at-the-world Blake Hunter.

"Maybe you should call the police."

"I did. I talked to the deputy sheriff. Ryan Tanner's so laid-back it's disgusting. He's no help. And, oh yes, I'm receiving anonymous thank-you notes from someone I fired or somehow pushed out of the company." She described the cards. "Olivia, are you still there?"

"Yeah, I'm here."

"Oh good. You were so quiet, I thought we had been disconnected." Amber continued to share all she had learned about the demented but vulnerable Joe, including traipsing through his family's cemetery, his living conditions, and extensive library.

"And there's the matter of the dead body in Joe's yard."

Amber pictured Olivia straightening her posture and replaying the last sentence in her mind to make sure she had heard Amber correctly.

"What?" Olivia said. "You're creeping me out. Whose body?"

"They haven't identified her yet but are sure she's not from around here. No clue about who she is or how she got here. All I know for sure is that she was wearing white sandals."

"Joe must be involved in some way."

Amber defended Joe, "There's a huge mystery surrounding Joe's family, but every time I'm with him, he's gentle as a newborn baby. I don't think Joe has a mean bone in his body."

"Doo ya...w'nt ad..vice?"

"No, I want to vent. For the moment, everything is in check. Except for the porch door to the deck that seems to be able to open itself." Amber recounted all the times the door was open when she had not opened it.

"I think you entered some twilight zone and need to get out of there this minute. Nothing is normal. Give up on this commitment and come back to LoDo. A dead body would be the last straw for most people, Amber."

"Don't go whacko on me. You're being a bit melodramatic. The body doesn't involve me. Everything does seem to be off plumb, but I'm not in a third-world country. People here, except for Blake Hunter, are civilized. Seeing Joe's situation firsthand was a real downer for me, took me by surprise, but talking to you has helped me get grounded again. There actually are a couple Western-type events during July in Westcliffe that I'm looking forward to attending. And from what I've seen, Joe's ranch is loaded with mystical rock formations. I'm heading there tomorrow to scout it out. I think the best is yet to come."

At seven thirty the next morning, Amber sat on the front porch, stroking Brutus.

"We can take our time today. In fact, I've packed a sandwich, and we'll make a day of it. Jeez, Brutus, get off my feet. You cause real pain."

Amber slung her backpack over her shoulder and led the way. Brutus stayed at her side. "This is quite unusual for you to not go running off. You act like you're unsure where we're headed. Well, guess what? I'm unsure too. I have no idea where we will end up."

They stopped at Joe's, and Amber gave him a bag containing lunch and told him she would be gone for most of the day. As they trudged past the shed, Amber said, "Someday, we are going to check out that shed, but not today. I want to see more of this magnificent property."

They came to a small meadow with an intriguing rock formation on the opposite side. Amber took long strides across the meadow and lumbered up rocks. From a number of perches, her sight could follow the meadow all the way to the Sangre de Cristo Mountains miles away. Amber studied the scenery in all directions and found it to have character. Besides the typical hills and valleys, rock formations in all shapes and sizes dotted the terrain like artistically placed tattoos.

"Finally, something that takes my breath away. I don't see a fence or even the remnants of one anywhere. This is probably not good ranch land, but it is exactly where I would build a home," she told the dog. "These rocks will be my favorite place to hike and climb." Amber spied a point at the summit of a very rocky formation that held promise for inspiration and worked her way to it. She found an indentation in a rock, took her book from the backpack, and leaned back. She read for hours surrounded by the majesty of the mountain scenery.

Brutus romped, disappeared, and reappeared until he tired himself and rested beside her. She looked up from her book, oblivious to the world around her. Her mind searched for something. The harder she concentrated, the more it eluded her. She grew tired of the hunt and drifted to the countryside that moved her into a trance where she longed to stay forever. The probability of being planted on a mountaintop for the rest of her life faded with the hours. Her practical side spurred her to get back to the cabin before dark.

They returned to the cabin and found the back door swaying in the breeze. She sighed and shut it. The excitement of returning to her special place tomorrow overshadowed any apprehensions.

Amber placed her breakfast dishes in the dishwasher and was wiping the countertop when Brutus cut loose with an intense barking spell and was silenced by a soothing deep-pitched voice. Amber was on her way to the front door when a spirited, steady rap on the door began. Amber opened the door. No one was in her line of sight, and she hesitated before stepping out of the cabin.

Amber turned toward the sound of a male voice talking to Brutus and was both surprised and relieved to discover Ryan seated in a rocker, petting the dog. He flashed a broad smile at Amber and continued to talk to Brutus.

"Hello, Ryan. Do you have news on the dead woman? Oh, I'm sorry, please come in."

Ryan stood, and Amber realized he was out of uniform. He was just as good-looking dressed in jeans and a dark-blue shirt with the sleeves rolled up to his elbows.

"No, there is nothing to report on the case. I just wanted to tell you that I talked to Blake about Brutus, probably didn't do any good, but you never know," Ryan offered.

"Did you interrogate him about the body? Blake Hunter is the only person in all of Westcliffe I've seen use a gun."

"What makes you think the woman died of a gunshot wound?" Ryan asked.

"I just assumed."

For the first time since they met, Amber saw a frown ensnare Ryan's features. His countenance shocked her and lead her to believe he might consider her a person of interest. They stood within inches of each other—but might as well have been miles apart.

Ryan broke the pause, "I'm heading up Mount Hermit. It's a fun ride on a bumpy road. Come with me. It's an adventure you need to experience at least once in your life."

"Oh, wow." Blindsided by the invitation, Amber stammered as she stalled for time to recover. "I guess I could…have nothing else going on right now. In fact, this is probably perfect timing. I do feel a need to get my mind on something else. It would be nice to put some distance between the crime scene and me, and I'd like to see more of the scenery around here. I've only ventured within walking distance so far." Amber regretted using the words *crime scene*. *What was I thinking? What is Ryan thinking?* She hoped he had not noticed. She chained Brutus, locked the cabin door, and climbed into Ryan's battered red pickup truck, strategically placing her feet to sidestep any fossilized food and trash on the floor.

"So many of the mountains in the ranges around here appear to be tall, almost the same height."

"Many are over 14,000 feet. We call them *Fourteeners*," Ryan explained.

Amber let the comment pass. She had lived in Colorado all her life and had spent considerable time in the mountains as a spectator in the natural playground. She knew a few things about the state's geography, high altitude, and local terminology.

Spread out at the foot of the peak like the flat campground around a teepee, they drove County Road 160, better known as Hermit Road, through the flourishing ranch land where open fields were vacant of trees except for those deliberately planted to shade houses and barns. They reached the base of the mountain and started the rapid ascent. A few miles up, they passed a turnoff to Lake Hermit. "I wouldn't mind walking around a lake," Amber suggested. "I find the sights and sounds of any type of water therapeutic."

But Ryan's truck chugged on up the mountain. "That'll be an excursion for another day. I'm not stopping until I get to the top," he said.

Amber lost sight of the scenery after the turnoff. She kept her eyes glued straight ahead for fear that moving a muscle or any shift in weight might push the truck over a ledge. On Ryan's side, the mountainside tumbled in a sheer drop to the ravines below. He concentrated and did not speak. With his booted foot, Ryan gingerly tapped the gas pedal, easing the truck over one deep washout in the road after another. Boulders popped up in the middle of the road, and he maneuvered the truck over them with the adeptness of stepping around them on foot. The mirror on Amber's door almost scrapped against the granite wall. She raised her hand to her mouth and gnawed on a fingernail until a sliver fell onto her sweatshirt. Her only consolation was that the steep drop-off was on Ryan's side, out of her full view. In most places the road was only wide enough for his truck. She had no idea how Ryan would handle an oncoming car. At ten thousand feet of altitude, they passed timberline, and the forested landscape became rocky terrain devoid of trees for the remainder of the incline.

After twelve miles of torture, they reached the summit. As Amber's feet touched ground, the magnificence of her surroundings dazed her, and she mechanically moved away from the truck to capture a full view of the Wet Mountain

Valley stretched out below. She walked into a bountiful field of wildflowers in purples, oranges, yellow-gold, and white, some as tiny miniatures that could only be seen by inspecting the ground as she walked. She picked a spot to lounge among the natural wonders; her legs draped gracefully to her side and basked in the tranquility and sights from the top of the world. Somewhere in her peripheral vision, she saw Ryan sit on the ground and wrap his extended arms around his knees. They imbibed, neither was breaking the silence—each lost in a welcoming disconnection from the rest of the world, and Amber's memory of the ordeals of the last few months evaporated into the literally thin air.

The essence of time took a leap off the mountain, leaving them suspended in the moment. The sun slid in and out of scattered clouds as if playing a private game of hide-and-seek. Two clouds joined together and floated across the sun. The diminishing light and change in temperature jolted Amber from her reverie. "Besides attempting suicide on mountainsides, what else do you do for fun?"

"Go to a movie when one is playing at the old Jones Theater. Sometimes, it has live performances, but I'm not too much into that. The building has an interesting and rather colorful past: used to be a saloon and pool hall during the mining heydays around here." He leaned back on an elbow. "I'm on a bowling team."

"Oh, yes, I noticed the bowling alley at the edge of town."

Ryan looked contemplative. "Hum, go to church on Sunday, that's about it."

"Regular attendee, huh?"

"Well, my father's the pastor, so don't have much choice." Ryan chuckled. "Just kidding, even if he weren't, it's the right thing to do."

"Your father's a preacher, and you weren't given a biblical name?"

"Actually, yes, I was. My full name is Matthew Ryan. My mom didn't want my name shortened, wanted me to be called Matthew, but my father said Matt was a better fit. They finally gave up disagreeing about it and settled on calling me Ryan. How about you? Is faith a part of your life?"

"I'm kind of an evolving Christian. Every time I think I have religion all figured out, it throws me a curve ball, and then I'm back to sorting it out again. My mom has always been pious, but a lot of what she preached never made sense to me. I'm still searching for my equilibrium with religion. I feel more spiritual than religious. But I'm a firm believer that everyone should take charge of her own life, go after what she wants, and make it happen."

"Seems to be working for you."

Amber was offended and confused by his comment. He had planted some seeds of uncertainty triggering that too familiar self-doubt and she wondered. *Does he agree that it is working for me, or is he questioning my state of affairs?* Now, she wasn't sure herself. She had custom-designed her world, and it had been perfect until this year. Her tranquility fled. She was tempted to bolt down the mountain on her own two feet. Agitation surfaced as a pout. She turned her face away and let her mind sift through the comment again and drew the same conclusion. Ryan was wrong. He was clueless. She would consider the source and let it go.

"Some unresolved mother-daughter conflicts?" Ryan pressed.

"What? I'm sorry. My mind drifted for a minute. What did you ask?"

"Some unresolved mother-daughter conflicts?"

"Maybe, but I think it's more that we just don't have much in common. She never worked outside the home and doesn't understand the demands of a career. She preferred that I have a husband rather than a boyfriend."

"So you have a serious boyfriend?"

"No, that's history. My mom's convinced that he didn't want a commitment, but I was the one who thought we had the ideal arrangement. The breakup with Todd was months ago."

"Sorry I asked. You look like you lost your best friend." Ryan sounded sincere.

"Best friend, soul mate, whatever descriptor you want to use."

"Where did you meet?"

"At work, of course. That's where I've spent all my time. He was with the company before I started. We actually met in the parking lot. Both going to our cars at the same time."

"Is that allowed? I mean being involved with a coworker?"

"It's a problem if you work in the same department. Todd was in marketing. Our offices weren't even on the same floor, and he actually changed companies a few years ago."

"Two corporate suit wearers."

"I guess that's a true statement, but it wasn't our careers that attracted us to each other. Todd and I had a relationship that worked. I was busy with my job, and he was busy with his job. Plus he had joint custody of his kids and was strapped with making child support and alimony payments. We enjoyed doing things together, all the activities and events around LoDo, day road trips. Getting involved in his previous life by marrying him would have made life so complicated for both of us. It just wouldn't have worked."

Amber suppressed the urge to tell Ryan how much she missed Todd. She missed going to the symphony or plays with him, or walking to Coors Field for a sporting event, or just walking the streets of LoDo. But she knew locking out the whole mess of emotions was the proper prescription for the moment and prevented further analysis.

"But I think my work bothered my mom more than my relationship with Todd. I can still hear the sermonette she delivered the last time we talked: 'Why not get a job with less responsibilities and hours? It's insane to be so devoted to something instead of someone. See what you get in return. No business is going to look out for you. You've got to follow God's will. Stop trying to take control.'" *Jeez, Mom, give me a break!*

Amber had wanted to scream. But she explained to Ryan, "I'm used to going it alone. You know what Thomas Jefferson said? 'Dependence leads to subservience.'"

"Well, we wouldn't want that, would we?" Ryan changed the subject. "You sound like a serious career woman. What did you do in Denver?"

"From the time I was young, I wanted to work in an office. I graduated from college with a degree in finance and accepted a job offer with a large HMO. It was my first and only interview. The first years, I worked a normal week while studying for my MBA. Once I had that, I started receiving promotions and special assignments. Of course, each required a few more hours. My workweek grew to fifty and then sixty hours. I didn't mind. Time was inconsequential. I loved my job. I learned the corporate culture and got swept up in its intrigue. The opportunity to associate with people who not only thought big, but also brought their decisions to fruition, was exhilarating and a real perk to me. My boss taught me scores of business applications, which was an education in itself. After years of learning and applying, I had reached a comfort level, a zone I didn't choose to leave. Sorry, that's way more info that you wanted to hear."

"Actually, I like knowing how other people live and what drives them. Your first passion was your work. Did you like living in the city?"

As Amber answered, she pictured the scenes in her mind. "Yes, I'd take long walks past Union Station, sip cappuccino in cafés, loved being a people watcher, studying them as they scurried on their way with a purpose in their steps. After being let go from my job, my assigned number of 'uno' made me feel like I was the only soul in Denver without an urgent calling, the only one stuck in a state of limbo."

"Why'd you leave something perfect and come to something rustic?"

"I was in need of long vacation—needed to take a break from all the elements of my life. I probably should have gone to an exotic island and sat on the beach all day. But simply put, I needed a change: change of pace, change of scenery, change in routine, and change in perspective. The list is endless."

"Well, have you had enough change yet?"

"Apparently not!" She laughed, and then the question struck a deeper humorous chord, and she went into a string of laughter. "I don't feel any different yet. But I've been doing all the talking. Let's put you under the microscope."

"Too bad, not enough time for that now. We need to head down the mountain."

Amber's grip was welded white-knuckled to the armrest as Ryan traversed down the mountain, holding her breath more times than she breathed. At times, she closed her eyes so she really couldn't tell she was on the drop-off side. The bottom was a long way down. Ryan's vehicle crawled over and around rocks in the roadway like a centipede. Any vehicle that goes up comes back more beat-up than when it started. No wonder Ryan's truck needed detailing, bodywork, and a paint job.

When safely back on smooth road again, Amber said her first words: "I'd hardly call that a road."

"I never get tired of that drive. It just brings something alive in me."

"Well, it scared the life out of me."

"How about stopping by my place for a beer?"

"I'm a prude that way, don't drink anything stronger than a cola. Never developed a taste for alcohol. I'm a workaholic teetotaler. But I'd settle for a glass of ice water. I think my throat is full of dust and dried out from sucking oxygen-deprived air."

"You've told me a little about your mom. Now, tell me about your dad."

Amber sighed. She knew she had to say something. "My dad died when I was a teenager. Mom was a homemaker who took care of the family. She replaced that purpose in life by delving into church activities. She is on every committee, attends every potluck, and spends many hours everyday at the church. It's really stuffy and boring. She met a widower named Ted there. My brother Trevor has only met Ted twice but can't stand him. Trevor says Ted is looking for a purse or a nurse. I think probably both. I don't think about it. It's her life. She can do what she wants. The whole dating thing is weird though. She seems happy. That's all that matters."

Amber was glad it was a short drive. She had shared more than she wanted. She realized she had gone off on her mom and not said anything about her dad.

Ryan's white clapboard house was located on Main Street at the edge of town. Homes on either side shared a similar style, and all were on minuscule parcels of land not much bigger than the houses. All would have been built a hundred years ago when families felt blessed to have three or four rooms and a roof over their heads. The structures were rectangular, and Ryan's had an addition on the back that was topped with a typical shed roof. The front yard was free of flowerbeds, plants, or shrubs, leaving a sickly lawn to spread from the sidewalk to the foundation. Ryan held the front door open for Amber, and she stepped into the living room. They walked down the center of the room, which was just wide enough for a two-person passage. The room was furnished with a television, sofa, and chair with one end table. Amber almost heard the bare walls begging for artwork. Through a doorway off one side of the room, Amber saw an unmade bed. A second door gave a view of a bathroom. Through a doorway at the far end of the room, they entered the kitchen.

Amber took a seat at the kitchen table. The small white pine table probably had doubled in weight over its lifetime with coat after coat of paint. Surface nicks and scars revealed shades of every color in the spectrum. One by her hand was sunflower yellow in the shape of a teardrop. Ryan had his head in the refrigerator when his phone rang. He ducked his head to clear the shortened back door and stepped outside to take the call.

When he returned, his face was flushed, and his manner ruffled. "I'm sorry. I'll have to give you a rain check on this happy hour. I forgot about an appointment. I'm really sorry. I apologize. I'm really sorry about this."

"Don't be sorry. I'd better get home to check on my problem pooch anyway."

Ryan drove the roads as if he were late for his wedding. The bed of the truck fishtailed around every bend in the road, and his carefree temperament morphed into that of a distracted maniac.

"Is this a new kind of sport, or do you have a real emergency? You know, it doesn't even matter. Either way, I'll walk from here. Just let me out!"

"Well, it's neither. I forgot that I had committed to going to Colorado Springs today. I'm already late. A few more minutes won't change anything. I guess. I'll see you get home safely."

Ryan dropped her off in the front yard and created a plume of brown dust as he hurried off. Brutus went crazy with excitement, barking and jumping around Amber. She took him off his chain and threw sticks for him to fetch. His retrieving was unreliable at best. Sometimes, he would bring the stick back; other times, he returned empty. But the exercise wore him down. Amber started to chain him when she heard something. She let the chain slide out of her hand and listened. The sound of that annoying but familiar whistle that followed her around Denver had made its way to Westcliffe. She kept her body planted but looked around without detecting a movement of any kind. With Brutus by her side, she hurried inside where she was summoned to the porch by the open back door.

FIVE

mber's favorite rock formation was the largest in the area. Her goal for the day was to get to its far side and see what lay beyond. She planned to devote the day to exploration of the glacial creation she had staked a claim to—declaring it hers. "I need to think of an appropriate name for this natural wonder. Something meaningful just to us, Brutus," she concluded.

She anticipated the hike could be a challenge and again, packed a sandwich for her and left one for Joe at his house.

She climbed over and around boulders and reached the far side by noon. She discovered a smaller meadow where nothing noteworthy made an impression except a steel building that reflected the sunlight like a giant flashlight. At first, she thought it must be another workshop. That theory disintegrated when she observed that the ground around its foundation lay naked and dark. And the shed was located about a mile from where the last pieces of the Stoners' vehicle inventory were strewn.

Amber could see freshly matted paths to the building, not an old nostalgic lane, as she would have expected of anything associated with Joe's property. Maybe the packed grass was from local ATVs. Ryan had mentioned that some ranchers used them to round up their livestock. Joe had no cattle. Perhaps recreational ATV users were taking liberties on his property.

"Brutus, this building has been recently constructed and is so far from Joe's. Joe can't walk this far, especially over such rugged terrain. I suppose he could drive his pickup, but from what I saw, his truck hasn't been out of the barn for months. Why would he put a building here? There isn't even a road to it. If that building had a window, we would hike over to it and take a peek."

Brutus's response was to let his tongue hang loose as he panted.

"Okay, you can have some water, and I'll have lunch. I'll read for a few hours, and then we'll head back."

Amber had packed a collapsible water dish for Brutus that she had found in a closet at the Grants. She shared half of the water in her bottle with Brutus and ate her sandwich. The full-circle vantage point of her perch stirred her. She took her book out of her backpack and placed it in her lap. Inspirational vistas crowded her on one side, and the quiet meadow freed her on the other. She read until her eyes begged for a break. She stared into the distance, mesmerized by the tranquility of the meadow.

A shiny spot appeared and crept through the center of the landscape. Amber squinted into the bright daylight to identify the movement. She reached into her backpack for her binoculars and raised them to her eyes. Bringing the target into focus, she saw the glaring object was the hood of a bumblebee-yellow pickup truck, luminous as a burst of radiant energy. It crept toward them as if the bed was full of eggs. As it came closer, Amber could see the bed of the truck was covered with a tarp.

Brutus jumped to attention just as Amber heard the buzz of another engine. She followed the sound and spotted a motorcycle speeding from another direction.

"Looks like we have company, Brutus. That's one aggressive rider. If he went any faster, he'd be flying."

The black motorcycle with overstated shiny chrome barreled toward the pickup. The rider's black helmet became one with the black cycle and created the image of a black streak in her sight. When he reached the pickup, he slowed almost to a stop. He revved his engine, popped the clutch, and the front wheel of the cycle reached for the sky, gripping the air as if it were a solid surface. The cycle held a perpendicular line to the ground as the back wheel spun, churning up and spitting out grass and soil. Just as quickly, the front wheel descended, and both vehicles sped to the building, braking hard to stop in front of a garage-type door.

"That was one showstopping wheelie," Amber whispered. "I guess it's silly to whisper. They can't see or hear us, Brutus."

A figure in blue jeans and T-shirt dismounted the cycle and walked to the building. He unlocked the door and lifted it up. The pickup was driven in, and the door was shut behind it.

"That can't have anything to do with Joe." Amber returned to her book.

Sometime later, the door opened, and the cyclist went to his Harley. He stuffed a small bag into the ornamented saddlebag astride the back wheel of his bike and rocketed his machine out a trail. The door to the building closed again.

"We better head home. We can solve this mystery another day. We're really in the dark, good buddy. Let's get you back to the cabin before you have heat stroke, or something else that would mortify me."

On the way they stopped to spend some time at Joe's. As she had many times, Amber went into the room with all the books and picked up an Abraham Lincoln biography off the desk that she had been reading to Joe.

Amber read a couple of chapters before Joe drifted off into a snoring, deep sleep. She returned the book to the desk and studied some of the other titles in the makeshift bookcases. Joe had arranged the books into categories of math, science, English, history, and literature. Although she suspected Joe had never been to a library, he had developed a similar system for organizing the textbooks and other various volumes. One crate held loose papers. Amber took a pile of papers to the desk, sat down, and thumbed though them. Some were handwritten poems. Some were receipts for purchases of equipment and cattle. In the middle of the stack, she found a handmade notebook made from tablet paper punched with a crude hole and tied together with a piece of yarn. It appeared to be a journal of some kind. She strained to read the beautiful, cursive letters written in pencil that were evaporating like invisible ink on yellowed pages. Deciphering would take effort and time.

I don't know which was more tiring, the trip across the ocean from Scotland or the train ride across the United States. If I had not been filled with excitement, I would be exhausted. Some passengers on the ship became ill and were very weak when we disembarked. Thanks be to God, I remained healthy. I arrived yesterday and just as he had promised in his letter, Luke and his parents met me at the station in Westcliffe. We went directly to a small church and were married by the minister. The church was a modest country church with a bell tower and tall steeple topped with a cross. From what I gathered, the community is very proud of it. I wore my prettiest dress on the train and tried to keep it from getting wrinkled. Mother made it for me especially for this occasion. Its emerald green color gave it a royal touch, and I received many compliments on it. It was late afternoon when our carriage pulled into the Stoner ranch.

America is beautiful, and I was completely amazed by everything I saw, the land, the people, and the opportunities. I'm so happy to be here and give thanks for my many blessings. My gratitude for an American man to send me the money to come to this wonderful land to be his wife will never end. And Luke is tall, dark, and handsome.

I had thought that I might make myself available to teach school here in the West. I mentioned it to Luke, but he said he did not want his wife working. He is right. There is no need. I will have my hands full being a rancher's wife.

The next page was blank, giving Amber the chance to track down Brutus. "Come, Brutus. Come inside where I can keep an eye on you."

Brutus followed obediently. "I'm shutting the front door. You'll be my hostage until I finish reading this one paper, and then we'll head home."

Amber read on.

It has been four months since I arrived. We live in the same house as Luke's parents. Luke is their only child, and they depend on him. He works very hard for them. He works harder than any other man I have ever met, and he never complains. His mother almost died when he was born and then could not have any more children. Luke's dad is a bit mean-spirited, and I am afraid of him. Life here is more primitive than I anticipated. The work is hard, and you are never done. Luke's mom and I are busy from sunup to sundown. Luke and his father come in for meals, but otherwise, are out ranching or repairing equipment in a shop out back. Winter will set in soon. Maybe we will have a day off to go into town or to church on a Sunday morning.

The next pages were blank. Amber turned until she found another entry.

Winter in the high country has been restrictive. Getting from the house to the barn is as far as we venture some days. I have been told that most winters are not as severe. Next year should be better. I have read all the books I brought with me; don't know what I would have done without them. I look forward to spring when we can go into town. Luke's mother has said we will go. Luke's father doesn't seem right in the head. Some days, he sits on the front step and stares at nothing. Other times, he talks to himself. A couple of times, he has disappeared and Luke had to go find him.

Again, Amber had to turn many blank pages before finding another paragraph. The entries were undated and appeared to be written in chronological order.

Luke's mother and I had a wonderful day in town. We chatted with a few ladies at the mercantile store. We picked out calico for new dresses and broadcloth for aprons. But most exciting was the baby flannel, lace, ribbon, and crocheting thread for our baby that is due in a few months. There were so many things to look at in the store. Luke's mother said we could come again before winter. She let me buy three books and said I could get three more next time. This is the kindest she has been to me.

On the last page, Amber found a short paragraph.

This was a very long and harsh winter. My birthday came and went and there was no mention of it by the Stoners. They do not take time to celebrate or enjoy any indulgences. I did receive greetings from home. It made me happy, but then it made me cry. I miss my family and friends. I wish I could spend some time with another woman my age. But our daughter Sarah was born, and it has been a blessing to have another person in the house. She has a sweet and sensitive disposition. New life should bring new beginnings. Luke's father wandered off without a coat and suffered some frostbite. His behavior is quite odd. Luke says not to worry.

Amber pictured Joe's mother as young and full of promise. She could feel the woman's hope slide away month by month. She never intended to violate the privacy of Joe's mother by reading her innermost thoughts. But, if his mother had bothered to write them, she wanted someone to read them. Amber was that privileged someone. With privilege, comes burden. His mother had chronicled events from her life for posterity before they could fade from her own memory. They were fading from the written word as well. Soon, they would be gone and forgotten.

SIX

Amber spent several hours each day over the next week perched in the rock high above the world. She devoted the remainder of each day to Joe. Once a day, she went to his house and read to him. She prepared him meals and jabbered to him about anything that came to her mind. Most often, he just listened. When he did talk, he expressed himself articulately, and they had lengthy conversations about the contents of his books. Amber noticed that while surrounded by his homemade library, Joe was tranquil and lucid. The farther he roamed from that room, the more confused he seemed to become and the less he spoke. And to her relief, he had not called her Sarah since that first time she had been inside his house.

Westcliffe had finally come through for her. The combination of a respite from a daily schedule and refuge from the world had Amber relaxed and able to enjoy the simple things. An old man and a huge dog dominated her life. Caring for and focusing on them was making her happy.

The day had come to investigate the workshop near Joe's house. Amber was determined to figure out why Joe looked like he would faint every time she mentioned the subject.

She and Brutus started out early and ventured off their usual path when the shed came into view. They plodded through knee-high grass and made their way to the door. The foundation of the shed was covered with vegetation. It did not look like anyone had entered it since Joe's dad died. A stand of ponderosa pines provided a natural break, protecting the structure from wind, snow, and sun. It looked like the most solid building on the property.

Amber turned the doorknob, and the latch released. "We're in luck, Brutus. It's not locked. I don't think this door has been opened in years. Let's give it a try."

With a push, the door swung open of its own volition, although the hinges screeched in protest. On the inside walls, two-by-four studs were exposed, as were the rafters. Fair-sized windows were centered on three of the walls and smaller windows flanked the door, allowing plenty of natural light to enter. A workbench extended from wall to wall across the back. Tools hung from nails in an orderly and precise fashion above the bench. A vice was mounted at one end of the bench and tin lard, coffee, syrup, and tobacco cans lined the back of the bench. Amber pried the lid off one can and found bolts. She tried another and found screws. Wooden boxes of small parts lined one sidewall where ropes, chains, and fan belts of different sizes peppered the wall. A potbelly stove stood centered on the other wall flanked by a couple of radiators leaning against the studs. Other than a few oil stains on the floorboards resided a heavy layer of dust and cobwebs everywhere; the shop was neat and organized.

"I'm totally lost, Brutus. This is a peaceful place. I feel like everything is under control in here. Why would the mention of it turn Joe inside out?"

Brutus pawed at a mousehole chewed between two floorboards, lost in oblivion in his pursuit of a sunken treasure. He dug ferociously at the wood as if it was dirt, and Amber's words fell flat upon the stale air.

"This shop belonged to a meticulous man, Brutus. Outside belonged to a different soul. I'm getting more confused than enlightened. There is nothing spooky, unusual, or sinister here."

Amber wanted to understand Joe's reaction. She went round and round the room—but sensed nothing. Determination pushed her further.

She snooped in all the tins and rummaged through all the boxes of parts. Her investigation into the inventory of typical mechanical components yielded more questions than clues. A sneezing spell forced her to surrender her quest. She retreated to the outside with Brutus at her heels like a shadow. She pulled the door closed and double-checked that it had latched.

"You know what, Brutus? We've taken in the gloriousness of this world on our sunrise walks. Today, let's go home and stay home. I would like to polish up my resume. I haven't opened my laptop since I came. I will stay out of cyberspace. My emails can pile up as high as one of these mountains. I don't care. But I should give some thought to a position with the nonprofit company where Olivia works. Olivia has been hounding me."

They returned passing Joe's house, crossed the road, and walked down the Grants' driveway.

"What do you think, Brutus? The foundation received funding for a director of operations position. Should I talk to the president? It doesn't have to be a formal interview. I could just troll, see what I snag."

Amber's mind raced through the troubling memory of a visit to the foundation when Olivia first became employed there. The place had something compelling about it in an odd sort of way: friendly and casual but unimpressive. The receptionist was taking messages on a tablet of paper bound by a binder clip. The paper itself was already used on one side and had been cut into fourths to make a notepad. Amber had sidestepped a fray in the carpeting. The obvious lack of corporate waste was intriguing, but the absence of prestige was a downer. She was held hostage by the visual image of the lobby of her own former workplace, with its bronze statues and the therapeutic calming effect of the wall waterfall. If she thought hard enough, she could hear the rapid click-clack sound of her heels against the marble floor as she had crossed it many times everyday. It was the sound of movers and shakers—the sound of success.

"I'm not sure I'm ready for that Brutus, better keep that one aside for now." But the pros and cons of working for a nonprofit played a game of ping-pong in the back of her mind.

A few days later, the duo set out on another pilgrimage to their seat in the natural setting. Although reaching her favorite spot was laborious, conquering the top was worth the effort. She had cut her climbing time in half, discovering the shortest and easiest route to the top. Amber was wrapped up in the plot and characters revealing themselves layer by layer in her novel. Her conscious mind chose not to acknowledge the intrusion of the Harley, but the roar of its engine snapped her to attention. She watched as the familiar motorcycle shot down the faint trail like a bullet and stopped so suddenly the backend of the bike came off the ground. The cyclist opened the door, and Amber quickly squinted through her binoculars in a futile attempt to see into the black abyss. Fifteen minutes later, the pickup made an appearance and entered the dark cavern.

"Darn, sure wish I knew what was in that building. Guys wouldn't drive all the way out here without a good reason. I find their presence distracting. I know we haven't been here very long, but let's go home."

Brutus scampered down the mountain like a climber rappelling off the rocks. He waited at the base of the rock formation for Amber to catch up.

Amber was at a loss for what to do next. Bored, restless, and eager for a change in venue, she stared out the kitchen window at six mule deer in the yard. One after another, they halted to nibble on grass or bushes. In complete synchronization, they all stopped and stood like statues. They gawked at her through eyes that looked like burnt holes in their heads. Their ears twitched as if they could hear her breathing. Without indication, they simultaneously took off on a run, gliding through the air. Their tiny hooves barely touched the turf. They were out of sight in the blink of her eye, leaving Amber alone once again. A rhythmic tap on the front door spun Amber on her heels.

As she opened the door, Ryan took one step forward and centered himself on the threshold, blocking Amber's sight to the outside. "Ready to blaze a trail?"

"I'm afraid to ask what that means." Amber felt her spirits soar at the prospect of an adventure with Ryan even though it might test her mettle.

Ryan stepped backward and to the side, giving Amber full view of the driveway. She spotted a horse on either side of her Jaguar; their reins tied to the side mirrors.

"Very funny. I'll give you that. I'll even give you credit for inventing such an original hitching post. The bad news is I'm not good at riding horses. I love watching other people ride. *Equestrian* and *cowgirl* aren't in my vocabulary. Horses and I don't like each other much."

Ryan laughed. They walked over to two classic specimens.

"Are these your horses?" Amber asked.

"No, I borrowed them from Blake. He has more horses than he needs. These two are my favorites. Whenever BJ and I went riding, these were our picks. This one's a palomino named Sam. That one's a thoroughbred named Sally."

Amber moved to Sally and reached to pat her face. The horse jerked her head out of Amber's reach.

"See how she is looking at me? She doesn't like me!"

"She reacted to the way you moved toward her. She doesn't know you, doesn't trust you, and senses you are uncomfortable and tense. Try to relax and talk to her on your approach."

Following his instructions, Sally let Amber move in closer and pet her head and neck. Amber spoke soothingly to the horse, and for a minute, the two tolerated each other. Sally raised her head and snorted.

"Those bulging eyes of hers are following my every move with great suspicion."

"You really are paranoid."

Holding the stirrup, Ryan coached, "Grab the horn of the saddle with your left hand. Put your left foot in the stirrup. As you pull yourself up, fling your right leg over the saddle."

"I know how to get on one. It's after I'm up there that things get out of control."

"Today will be amusing, if nothing else."

"Look how tall they are. I find their size very intimidating. I'd rather look down on them than have them looking down on me. I'd be okay on a little Shetland pony."

"With your long legs, that would be an amusing sight. You belong on this sleek, graceful beauty. Throw away your inhibitions for a few minutes and give it a try. Besides, the feeling is mutual. Sally isn't comfortable with anything above her head either. Just stand by her while we talk for a few minutes. Riding is a skill. Not everyone is a natural, but anyone can learn to do it."

Amber teased, "Is this horseback riding 101? Am I supposed to take notes, Professor?"

"Think of how difficult it was to learn to ride a bicycle. If you didn't lean with the bike, you lost your balance, and both you and the bike fell over. Balancing on a horse is simpler because the horse isn't going to fall over. It should be easier and less work than riding a bike."

"But the bicycle stops when I stop pedaling. I'm used to mechanical stuff. I put my foot on the brake. The car stops. A horse has a mind of its own."

"You've encountered many people with minds of their own and figured out how to get along. Why should an animal stump you?"

Amber and Ryan made eye contact. "I'm not going to admit that you're right," she confessed. "So Sally is a thoroughbred. She is beautiful, and her color is so rich. She looks like a varnished chestnut."

"Quarter horse to be exact. Let me show you how talented she is." Ryan mounted Sally and demonstrated how she could do a quick start from a stand still and could round tight turns, moving like liquid mercury.

"They're the fastest horses in the world over a quarter of a mile," Ryan said as he slid off Sally and handed the reins to Amber. "Time to saddle up."

He was on Sam and out the lane by the time Amber managed to get herself into the saddle. He waited for her on the road. "You're not riding a turtle. We'll be gone a week if you don't speed up."

As she followed Ryan down the road, Amber studied the man and the horse. The powerful cream-colored coat of the palomino was accented by a white mane and tail. There was a picture-perfect match between man and horse. Amber couldn't believe that Ryan looked even better on a horse than he did behind a sheriff's badge.

Starting out slow and easy, the horses walked a pace to allow Amber time to pick up the four-beat rhythms. Without any signal from Amber, Sally advanced to a trot, trying to jolt Amber out of balance. Amber applied Ryan's theories and stayed in the saddle. Seeing the countryside on horseback presented a new perspective, and as she relaxed, she started to enjoy it. Meanwhile, Ryan rode circles around her. She ignored him. Brutus frolicked nearby, sometimes behind them, other times in front. By lunchtime, Amber welcomed being back on her own two feet.

They stopped in a grassy area. The horses grazed, and Brutus stretched out for a nap. Ryan opened a saddlebag and hauled out a lunch of ham and cheese sandwiches on rye bread, apples, and candy bars. He even remembered a cola for Amber and a doggy treat for Brutus. Ryan and Amber each sat on rocks about the right size for stools and ate.

"So, first, tell me about losing your job," Ryan said.

"It's kind of a long story. Let's talk about something else." Amber chose to leave the painful scene buried for now. Talking about it to just anyone would be impossible. The memory of confiding in Olivia streaked through Amber's mind. It had been difficult to share even with her best friend whose reaction Amber could predict. It was hard telling what someone unfamiliar with her as a person and as an employee would think. She preferred not to go there.

"What's your bowling average?" she asked.

"Why, do you want to go bowling? Do you even know how to bowl?"

"Heavens no, well, yes. I mean, no, I don't want to go bowling, and yes, I tried it once and found my succession of gutter balls extremely boring."

"I love to fluster you. Are you having trouble finding your articulate self?"

Amber stared at Ryan without replying.

"I intend to sit here until you spit it out," he said.

Amber bit her lip as the torturous recall of every word flooded back to her. She remembered herself perched on the edge of a chair in Steven Kern's office, feeling numb yet fearing she might faint. Her mind had frozen as it searched its memory bank, looking for instructions on what to do. Of course, the bank was empty. She had never been fired before. She had felt a sudden rush of pressure in her head and raised a limp hand to her burning cheek. She had contemplated whether to take flight or lunge across Steven's desk, grab his Armani lapels, and shake some sense into his flawed thinking. She had done neither.

Turning to face Ryan, she said, "Well, the conversation with my boss went something like this: 'Amber, you know how I feel about you and your work. You're everything a company could ask for in an employee. Upper management knew if they wanted a project done correctly to give it to you. I fought hard for you, but in the end, no matter how valuable you are to the department, all directorial positions at your level have been eliminated. There's an immediate hiring freeze.' Blah, blah, blah. He spoke these words in his usual matter-of-fact tone. Until that moment, I had considered Steven handsome with his dyed black hair and big dark eyes, but he morphed into ordinary before my eyes."

"This came out of the blue? You had no forewarning?"

"Maybe I was blind."

Amber thought of Todd. The breakup was a surprise and out of the blue. One minute, their relationship was on track, and the next, it was upside down in the ditch. Corporate downsizing was more predictable. Amber realized she had a false sense of immunity and certainly would not have expected both events in a short time frame. Once she felt confident in both situations, she had neglected to pay attention and took both for granted. The more she thought about it, the more she knew in her heart—both were needed to sound a wake-up call to her.

"The business world is always in a state of flux, so you kind of get used to periodic bombshells. I got too comfortable, lost touch with the reality that the business climate could affect me. There were the company-wide indicators. For example, for many years, the company Christmas party was held at one of the big hotels in Denver, a sit-down dinner with a band and dancing and awards and bonuses. A few years ago, cutbacks were made with something else slashed each season. Last year, employees were given a fifty-dollar gift certificate, end of story. No party, no bonuses, no money spent on fostering relationships among working groups or showing appreciation for the individuals who contributed to the company's overall success. The biggest red flag

I missed was no new projects were coming my way. Cutbacks, yes, I anticipated, understood, and accepted, but my job—never."

Ryan studied her before offering, "Have you considered that it maybe was time to move on?"

"I suppose, but most troubling was it made me think about the people I had fired. I never liked it but did consider it necessary. Only a few failed under my direction, and each dismissal was a joint decision between upper management and me. But after jumping through one procedural hoop after another, ultimately, I became the scapegoat with both sides equally distrustful of me. Caught in the middle, I was cast as the enemy, the bad guy. But that went with the territory."

"I'm having trouble picturing you as the hatchet man."

The comment ignited an internal chuckle deep in Amber's psyche. Against her strongest resistance, she was captivated by the way Ryan's eyes danced when he was in a playful mood.

"Everything I did, I did because I thought it supported the interest of the company, and I bought into Steven Kern's philosophy: 'If you are in management and don't have two or three arrows in your back, you probably aren't doing your job.'"

Amber's thoughts drifted back to that day. During her passage from Steven Kern's office to her own, the people and fixtures in her vision had faded into shades of sepia. The aroma of coffee brewing at the coffee center usually caused her to take a deep breath, but the stimulating smell fell flat on her senses. Voices had called her name as she made her way to her office, but she had been ensnared in a silent web.

"I imagine you cried buckets once alone in your office."

"Probably should have—but didn't. I had a reputation to maintain, one of being a critical thinker, always rational and logical, the quintessential examiner of the facts. I think I was pragmatic to a fault. I understood the corporate world. I just felt immune from the radical adjustments necessary for correction. I held my head high, and after my exit interview, I made a beeline to my car."

Amber's matter-of-fact manner reappeared, and she relived going to her car that day. She recalled how sound had outrun sight when she heard the annoying whistle close by again. It was an amateur attempt at a melody that she could not discern. Just like all the other times, when she had looked around, there was no one there.

"That doesn't sound so bad, no politics or vindictiveness. With your background, you'll have no problem finding another job." Ryan surprised her with his own homegrown wisdom.

"I know. I just dread starting over, especially with the basics like learning everyone's extension, who does what, who to go to for certain things. It takes a while to learn the everyday stuff before you can concentrate on the big stuff."

"I have a feeling you'll do fine." Ryan was more suited as a cowboy than a businessman, but his naïve confidence in her was touching. At this point, he had given her more genuine encouragement than anyone else in her life.

"Somehow, now, I feel like a whiner. Good grief! I've been wallowing in self-pity. It probably is time to move on."

Ryan summed the whole episode up in a few words: "Things happen for a reason, and the main reason is it is time to move on. Don't read more into it than is there."

They continued to exchange ideas and viewpoints, and Amber found the simple philosophy from a guy who lived a down-to-earth life renewing. She shared more conversation with Ryan while seated on that rock than she had previously with any other soul. She could have stayed in that peaceful spot for hours. Meanwhile, Brutus had entertained himself by scouting out every scent he could follow and was ready to head back.

Rather than return on the same seldom-used road full of ruts, washboards, hills, and switchbacks, they went cross-country. Ryan rode beside her, and she asked, "Please tell me about Blake's son."

"There isn't much to tell. He left Westcliffe and doesn't care to return. Most people don't know where he is. I do, but we don't talk much."

"Why not? Weren't you friends?"

"Yes, but I want to give him all the space he needs. He knows what's right for him."

"Space from what?"

"Oh, these ranching families have a tendency to pass the ranch from generation to generation. BJ was just kind of fed up with ranching. He wants to see what else is out there, what life is like somewhere other than Westcliffe."

Amber was silent as she pondered the reality of BJ's situation. She had to agree. He should follow his heart and find his passion in life. He and she were in the same boat. Nothing in her current situation qualified her as an authority on life.

They rode into a small valley and were blinded by a bold reflection. They sidestepped out of the path of the rays and trotted toward the source. As they approached, the sight of a car jammed into some scrub oak came into view. They galloped up to the vehicle and dismounted. Amber held the horses while Ryan inspected the car. The abandoned car showed no physical damage, and whoever left it had done a poor job of hiding it. There was nothing unusual inside the car, and the registration papers were inside the glove compartment.

"I wonder if this could belong to our unidentified body," Ryan said as he looked over the papers. "The car is registered to a Melanie Carter."

Amber grabbed Sally's saddle and pressed her forehead into it as her mind whirled like a ceiling fan set on high speed. She closed her eyes to stop the spinning. When she opened them, Ryan was supporting her and calling her name.

Her mouth went dry, and she struggled to whisper, "Melanie used to report to me. Unfortunately, she is one of the people I fired."

Ryan used his cell phone to arrange to meet the sheriff at Blake Hunter's ranch. On the ride back to the Blake's ranch, Ryan was silent and preoccupied. Amber remained in the safety of a mental fog, blocking out all thoughts and awareness of her surroundings.

She arrived home somehow and rested on the sunporch, with Brutus at her feet and Joe by her side. When she opened the door in answer to a knock, it was déjà vu. But this time, Ryan and Gavin talked to her on the front porch.

"I understand you knew Melanie. When was the last time you saw her?" Gavin asked.

"I haven't seen her in months, actually more like a year or so. But I have been receiving anonymous thank-you notes from someone I fired. I can show you the first one that I received. I got so annoyed by them that I have thrown most of them away unopened."

Amber quickly stepped to the kitchen and returned to the open door. She handed Gavin the thank-you note.

"Just how angry was she over her dismissal?" he asked.

"Pretty average. Nothing alarming," Amber answered without hesitation.

"Would she have any reason that you know of to be in this area?"

"I don't know. I don't know! I certainly didn't give her my address. I've had my hands full with Joe. Somehow, he can open the back door to the sunporch. I find it open all hours of the day and night. It's like having a two-year-old around." Amber fought back the flood of tears welling up inside her.

"Why didn't you tell me you were having a problem with Joe? You can't have him opening your door," Ryan said.

"I knew everyone would overreact and think the worst of him. I've learned to cope with it. It's just one of his quirks. The back door is open some mornings and shut on others. There is no rhyme or reason that I can determine. Nothing is disturbed, and Brutus never barks."

Amber released the tears as she watched the lawmen drive away. Two hours before, she had been in a good place and filled with renewal. Now, she had depleted her arsenal of coping skills and knew a tension headache was brewing.

Amber brought Brutus in for the night, just as she had done on most nights, and gingerly lowered herself into a bubble bath. The warmth relaxed her stiff muscles, and she drifted into a peaceful zone. One sharp bark brought her straight up. She sat motionless as if she had been sprayed with starch, suspending even the blink of her eyes. She waited for more sounds. Hearing none, she wrapped herself in a terry bathrobe. From the dresser, she grabbed a brass vase and crept down the stairs. Amber hesitated on each step like a trained agent entering a suspicious crime scene. She eased herself to the sunporch and checked the back door. It was closed and locked. She sighed, relaxed her arms, and let them resume their normal position, but the fingers on her right hand retained their tight grip on the vase. As she reentered the living room, she conducted a visual search for Brutus and found him asleep on the floor by the fireplace.

"Crazy dog. Probably tried to catch a fly." She shook her head and headed to the loft. Amber put the vase back in its place and went to the window in hopes of being awed by a star-studded sky. But the sky was ebony, unlit by any heavenly bodies. She had never witnessed such darkness.

In bed, she glanced once more out the window and saw two parallel white spots as headlights raced along the distant road. *This isn't the city where people never sleep. It's the country. The sidewalks get rolled up at sundown. Where would someone be speeding to at this time of night?*

Amber was counting sheep when, without warning, a few large raindrops pelted the window. Within seconds, the splats against the pane exploded into a torrent of rain, slamming against the cabin. It ended as quickly as it began, like shutting off a faucet. She welcomed the quietness and drifted off to sleep. Numerous times during the night, her body spasmodically jerked as she dreamed she was slipping off Sally and tensed as she grabbed the pommel to break her fall. But something more serious had her tossing and turning, it was a vague feeling that things here were not right.

In the morning, Brutus cocked his head and watched Amber descend the stairs. She walked stiff-legged and said "Ouch" on each landing. Her first mission was to check the sunporch door. Finding it shut but unlocked met her expectation.

She shuffled to the front door. "Oh boy, Brutus. We won't be walking very far today. If you think this is funny, wait until you see me try to sit down. Being on horseback when you're not used to riding causes an old-fashioned case of saddle sore. That was quite a downpour we had last night. If a cabin could drown, this one should've."

Amber opened the front door, and Brutus bolted outside, brushing against her leg as he passed. She took a couple steps onto the porch to watch Brutus frolic and felt mud oozing between her toes. She frowned and walked off the porch into the damp grass to clean her feet.

"Now, how did all that mud get on the porch? Joe the Night Wanderer, what are we going to do with him Brutus? I'm glad he didn't leave this mess on the sunporch."

SEVEN

As Amber hiked, she concentrated on finding an appropriate name for her perch—one that encompassed all its earthly features. Word after word surfaced and was rejected. By the time she reached the top of the rock formation, she was out of words. Brainstorming had been one of her strengths; something she did without effort. The frustration of struggling with this exercise in combining vocabulary and creativity concerned her.

"I may never find the right word, Brutus. Have I lost my mental sharpness, or am I just out of practice? Or is there too much going on? My mind feels fried. I'm going to sit here in my spot and engage in mindless meditation, see if I can clear my head and reach a more creative level."

Brutus lay on his belly and rested his head on his front paws.

"Sometimes, you're just too cute. You probably think all this thinking is boring."

She sat in her spot in silence and let her mind look to the heavens. Out of nowhere, a menacing thought invaded her bliss. Recollections of Warren crept through her mind's eye. She fought to keep them buried, but they headed down the path to her consciousness before she could stop them. Since he had quit his job in her department, she had not seen or heard from him. It was her understanding that he went on to something better, and the parting was amicable. From what she remembered about his personality, he would never put the effort into writing her thank-you notes.

Warren had been a personal disappointment to Amber, although she had tried every career development plan available to help him be successful. She had worked with him one-on-one as a mentor and had sent him to training seminars. He was capable when he applied himself, which he could switch on and off. No matter what she tried, Amber failed to influence his behavior of waltzing in late, taking sick days often, endless personal calls, and browsing the internet. At first, he had been eager to please and insisted on working extra hours. He appeared to be going overboard to try and be accommodating and useful. Some unknown force had spun him 180 degrees, and he became cynical, defiant, rude, and developed a real you-can't-tell-me-what-to-do attitude. He refused to stay focused and refused to take his career seriously. If he had not resigned on his own, Amber would have placed him on probation. She remembered the relief she felt when he left voluntarily. She had personally hired him as her assistant, but his work ethic drifted off the chart. Amber considered herself a skilled judge of character on and off the job. She hated psychological guessing games, hated wasting her time on assumptions, hated grasping for the truth or for facts that would lead to the truth, hated the exhaustion of it all.

The conflict and sense of failure depressed Amber. Warren had been the first person she met that stumped her. She had been unable to figure out how to work with his personality type. He changed from a copycat to an odd duck in a short time. She pushed Warren out of her head. In the grand scheme of her life, he was a nit.

"I must say, good buddy, I'm pleased that a week has gone by without any activity at the steel building. I should mind my own business. It's not like we aren't tangled up in a few other mysteries. But before I can let it go, I must try to figure out what is going on over there."

They climbed down the backside of the rock formation, walked to the building, and tried the door, which was locked. At the back of the building, a small utility door was also locked.

"Not one window in the whole place. Whatever is inside will remain a mystery," she reported to Brutus.

As she rounded the corner of the building to head back to her perch, she heard the roar of the motorcycle. She darted back to the side of the building, squatted, and put her arm around Brutus, pulling him close to her side. She stroked his neck and chest to keep him silenced and under her control.

The Harley went silent except for the rhythmic *tinking* of the engine cooling. And then Amber heard the *purr* of the pickup truck engine as it idled. She peered around the corner and saw a short guy swing himself out of the cab of the truck. He exchanged a few words with the biker and folded back the tarp, covering over the truck bed. The routine replayed with the pickup entering the building, except, this time, the door was left open.

Amber retreated a few steps. "What a bummer! We were close enough to hear their voices but not close enough to make out the words. Brutus, this is one time you must listen and obey. You stay put, don't move a muscle. I need to steal one look inside the building."

She tiptoed to the edge of the door. The men were easing a cobalt blue Harley down a ramp off the truck. In the bed of the truck, another motorcycle rested on its side like a gutted buck during deer season. Spoke wheels, handlebars, chrome mufflers, and other cycle parts covered the floor of the building and workbenches. Two more complete bikes were parked at the far end.

She slipped back to Brutus. "Good boy. Your listening skills are improving. I don't know much about motorcycles, except that I can recognize a Harley when I see one, but I think we have a chop shop going on here. We might as well get comfortable because there is no way we can make it to the rocks without being seen."

Amber jerked when Brutus, for no reason, let out a yelp. She waited to see if they had been detected, but the clank of metal was all she heard. Her heart pounded in her chest long after the miscue. She sat down on the ground to wait it out, and Brutus put his head in her lap and snoozed. She reverted to thinking of a name for her spot with no better outcome. A thousand needles stabbed her foot. She guided Brutus off her legs and whispered, "I need to stand up and get some circulation going."

Amber hobbled around in a small square. She tapped her thighs as a signal for Brutus to come. They walked to the back of the building and looked for an escape route. The meadow lay flat and open in all directions, except the rock formation, which was in direct sight line of the open garage door. They would have to walk in the open and then circle back. Amber concluded it too risky and sat down to wait. Night was beginning to settle in when the pickup and motorcycle drove out of the shed. When all sounds of the cycle and pickup were gone, Amber started toward the rock formation.

She and Brutus were within twenty yards when, out of nowhere, the motorcycle raced back behind them. She stopped and turned to face the cyclist in a black helmet. Brutus stood motionless at her side. The motorcycle ripped toward them. When the cycle was within yards of them, she and Brutus split. Amber darted to one side of the cycle, and Brutus to the other. Brutus raced along side the cycle, barking as consistently as the drone of the engine. Amber ran for the rocks. The cycle wheeled around and chased Amber. Within arm's reach, the cyclist rode a circle around her. Then he did the same to Brutus. Suddenly, he turned, and the rider rocketed out of the meadow.

Amber ran to the rock formation and hustled until she got to the top. She stopped only when she reached her spot. Her muscles burned, and she gulped for air. "I don't know about you,

Brutus, but that took a decade off my life. The good news is he was just trying to scare us." She sat in her spot until she had the strength to head back to the cabin.

It was dark when they got home. Amber shivered from the chill of the night air. She slipped into a bulky sweater and paced the floor to warm herself. After lighting a fire in the stone fireplace, she sat cross-legged on the floor. A log popped with a kettledrum boom and awakened Amber from her trance. She sighed, went to the front door, flipped the dead bolt lock, opened the door, and faced the still blackness.

"Brutus, Brutus, Brutus, come boy. Brutus, come." Amber heard the thud on the porch floor planks as Brutus's paws landed. He barked a greeting and waited at her feet. She unleashed his collar from his chain and explained, "I need you inside tonight. I now have the burden of knowledge, and it's going to take this night to figure out what I should do about it."

EIGHT

Amber holed up in the cabin on a self-imposed time-out for another week and managed to escape any new drama. She only left for walks with Brutus and visits to Joe's. She was finding it harder and harder to occupy her time. Joe and Brutus weren't great conversationalists. She had overdosed on reading and had polished everything in sight—including her Jag. She itched for some form of entertainment, and Westcliffe was set to host one of its biggest events of the year. In the post office, she had read a flyer advertising the annual Westcliffe Stampede; a weekend that included everything from a pancake breakfast, a dance, a parade, kids' rodeo to a cowboy church.

The rodeo and parade scheduled for the day piqued Amber's interest. Designer jeans, a white blouse, and loafers were as Western as she could get, but she wasn't concerned about fashion. She bounced down the stairs hardly touching each step and got the jump on Brutus. Before he could mug her with his exuberance, she wrapped her arms around his neck and gave him a hug. She sailed through all the morning chores, compelled by a need to get going. The endless azure sky and fresh mountain air beckoned her to come out and stay out. The thought of being in town all day, roaming with strangers, experiencing some foreign activities added a touch of grace to her movements. She drove the stretches of roadways through God's country, with Joe in the passenger seat. She took pleasure in giving him an opportunity to view the bigger world: an experience she felt he should have had as a child.

"This day is about eighty years overdue, Joe. You're going to love every minute of it. It's never too late to live life to its fullest."

Joe watched out the passenger seat window, scanning the countryside. Amber stole a glance at him and thought he appeared to be more like a ten-year-old boy than an old man with one foot in the grave. Two weeks ago, she had taken him to Pueblo and bought him new jeans, a blue plaid cotton shirt, and black leather shoes. She had decided that the thick hair of this near centurion deserved a salon cut too. He looked dapper in his outfit, and his hair was, not only combed, but also was staying in place.

They arrived early and took a stroll up one side of Main and down the other to scout out a good place for viewing the parade. The field at the end of town had more RVs parked on it than Amber had ever seen in one place. Noise, activity, and Main Street swarming with different kinds of people revived something in her that had been in a coma for too long. Excitement and anticipation radiated through town, and Amber fell right in step with the hustle and bustle.

Joe, on the other hand, walked at a snail's pace and recoiled behind Amber with each approach of a person from the opposite direction. Amber took his arm to keep him at her side.

"Joe, you're quivering like a frightened puppy. It's okay. You're fine. I'm not going to let anything happen to you. I know you have never seen so many people in town, but they're here to have fun. And that's what you and I are here for too. Relax. You tell me if you need anything. First, we're going to watch a parade. We'll just take one thing at a time. I think you'll like it."

Some passersby went their merry way, absorbed in their own agendas. Others took long looks at Joe and Amber. Amber blew them off, but then, the inevitable happened. As they passed the post office, Vera stood on the lawn huddled with two ladies.

"Amber, why would you drag Joe into town on a day like today?" Vera said.

The question took Amber by surprise. She looked at Joe who studied the ground as if he had done something wrong. Flabbergasted, she responded, "Why not?"

Amber kept her mouth shut. Her hand remained on Joe's arm, and she guided him along; his pace was now a hobble. Within earshot, the snide remarks accosted her and cut like a dagger.

"Imagine, a woman like her carrying on with someone Joe's age."

Determining who spoke the words was inconsequential. Amber was beyond caring.

"What a bunch of old biddies," she said.

A faint hee-hee came from Joe that made Amber laugh as well.

"Joe, I'm not sure if walking away is a mature way to handle this, but I do know that words usually bounce off narrow-minded people. Getting them to see another perspective is impossible."

Amber chose the charming Main Street Bed and Breakfast as their location for the parade. Its homey appeal and Victorian charm added a traditional feel to the otherwise Western character of the town. All the storefronts along Main Street had been renovated to original, a step back in time, yet fresh—a mixture of warm character and old West ruggedness. It was plausible that they could catch a glimpse of Wyatt Earp, Jesse James, or Buffalo Bill riding down the center of the street.

The parade began with promise. The high school band marched to the beat of the drum followed by a float and rodeo queens on prancing horses. Joe was wide-eyed when the old fire engines rolled by. It turned out to be the shortest parade Amber had ever seen, which was just as well. By the time the color guard passed, Joe was pacing around on the grass in front of the B&B and mumbling to himself.

After the parade, they walked around the rodeo grounds. Amber explained about the rodeo events. She could feel him tense up every time a cowboy strutted by. The sun beat down in earnest, and Joe moved slower and slower.

"Joe, you don't seem to be enjoying any of this. Do you want to go home?"

"Home, yes, home."

With a heavy heart, Amber drove Joe home and walked him into his house. "You rest awhile. I'll see you later."

Amber returned to her Jag and sat for a minute while she debated if she should return to town or crawl back into her cocoon. So far, the day had been one big disappointment and she held little hope for anything more. She turned on the ignition, wheeled the car around in Joe's yard, and stopped at the intersection of Joe's driveway and the road.

I'm not going to let a few old hens ruin my day. Then she spun onto the road.

Amber parked her car and walked to the rodeo grounds. Mutton bustin' was about to begin for the children. She bought a cola and headed to the stands. From somewhere in the crowd, she heard Ryan call her name. She spotted him and moved through the crowd. When they faced each other, she noticed a lady at his side. The mother of pearl buttons on the lady's red Western-cut shirt looked like gemstones reflecting the intense high-mountain sunrays. Her jeans were so tight that if she had a freckle anywhere on her hips or thighs, it would be albino by now. The legs of the jeans flared over Italian leather boots. The toes were pointed enough to pick ice. Her long witch black hair fell loose across her back like strands of silk, and her head was topped with a black felt cowboy hat. Designer sunglasses concealed her soul, but Amber felt a draft and kept her distance. Two young girls fidgeted at the lady's side.

"Amber, I didn't expect to see you here. Didn't know you were ready to mingle with crowds," Ryan said. "This is Meredith and her daughters Emily and Macy."

Amber took the obligatory step forward and extended her hand to Meredith who placed a limp red-tipped claw into Amber's. "It's nice to meet you. I'm from Denver and just here watching the Grants' cabin for the summer. Well, more realistically, watching their dog."

Meredith uttered "Ump" and moved her sight line beyond Amber.

"It's certainly a beautiful day, not a cloud in the sky. I saw a flyer for the stampede, and I can't resist a parade. I'm not sure about the rodeo, but I'm giving it a try. Are you girls going to participate in the mutton bustin'?"

The two small Meredith replicas simultaneously looked at Amber—as if she had two heads and wrinkled their noses.

"That'd be the last thing on Earth they'd want to do," Meredith said.

"Oh, I thought it sounded like fun, but I'll admit—I don't know what it is."

Ryan explained, "It's pretty simple. It's the kids' version of a bucking bronco or bull riding. Kids over seven years old try riding sheep. The one who stays on longest is the winner."

"Well, I definitely want to see that," Amber said.

Meredith locked her arm in Ryan's. "Sweetie, I just can't have the girls in this much sun, and you said you were starving. We just can't have you going hungry now, can we?"

Amber felt her cheeks burn, and she walked away as she completed her sentence: "You all enjoy the rest of your day."

She wove her way through the crowd and maintained a long stride until she reached the stands.

The mutton bustin' was cute. The kids were cute. The sheep were cute. Amber had enough cute and went back to Main Street to browse some shops until time for the rodeo. In a photo gallery, she found a picture of a field chock full of wildflowers. The chiming bells, larkspurs, lupine, and Indian paintbrush flowers displayed every color of an artist's palette. A panoramic view of the Sangre de Cristo Mountains in the background stood like a mighty force. The grandeur of the scenery spoke though the artist's brush. The painting was perfect for a stub of a wall by the balcony of her condo. Stick with the pristine native world, and she would never have to embellish or lie. People lie. Nature is what it is. Amber bought it and asked the shop owner to hold it for her until after the rodeo.

On the corner of Fourth Street and Main, she walked through a grassy area with benches, which according to the literature she had picked up at the visitor's center, had been donated as a park. On one bench, a couple of kids licking fast at ice cream cones squirmed to stay ahead of the drips. Blake Hunter sat alone on another bench, and Amber happened to be in the mood to talk to him. She debated taking some time to rehearse what to say. That seemed silly. She should be able to have a congenial conversation with this man. At least it should be easier with him sitting down.

"Mr. Hunter, I'm glad to see you here today. I have a couple of questions to ask you. Do you mind?" Putting the boldest look on her face she could muster, Amber took a seat on the other end of the bench.

Dressed in a chambray shirt and khaki slacks, Blake had lost the cowboy persona, and Vera's opinion proved to be more right than wrong. Dressed up and not scowling, he had some handsome features. A slight nod of the head was the only acknowledgement he gave her. Being dignified or rational while in his presence required a certain kind of raw skill or charm that, if Amber possessed, she had never tapped. She sensed he was deliberately ignoring her. She straightened her back, hesitated a minute, and then dove in.

"I've heard that your family and the Stoner family were the original homesteaders to settle the two ranches. That's quite a distinction. I'd love to hear some of the ranch's history. I'm fascinated by the connection between people and places."

Amber searched for the right words to continue with a one-sided dialogue while trying to bait Blake into the conversation. She spoke of the beauty of the setting and how surprised she was to see so many houses springing up miles from town.

"I think there must be no greater satisfaction for a rancher than to see his life's work pass on to his children and grandchildren. That's got to be comforting as he becomes elderly."

Blake turned his head toward Amber. And for a split second, she thought she had struck a chord with him? Then, their eyes locked and sent a fright through her. His hazel marbles provided no clue as to whether he was friend or foe. He spoke, "The Hunter ranch was granted to my family in 1875 by the U. S. Government. It's one of the biggest in the valley at about two thousand acres. I run thousands of head of cattle every year, just as my grandfather and great grandfather did. All these years, the Hunter ranch has been successful. There's a certain amount of pride in being a rancher. Ranchers made this valley what it is today. The Stoner ranch is much smaller, a few hundred acres. They shunned progressiveness, seemed to want time to pass them by. They were a hardworking family, but their operation was too small to amount to much. And luck was never on their side."

Blake Hunter had given Amber more information than she thought him capable of conveying. Maybe he really could provide a better glimpse of Joe.

"Did you know Joe's family very well?"

"We weren't in the same social circles, if you know what I mean. The Stoners' property has always been an eyesore. I can honestly say I have never set foot on their soil."

"That's amazing. Living so close and yet not acting as neighbors. How sad." Amber intended to make a statement and regretted adding an opinion. She felt as if she were walking on a bed of bees. Where to step or not to step presented a challenge. For her to figure out which words would cause him to stomp away seemed impossible. It had been a long time since she had had to work so hard at conversing with someone.

"There never was an occasion," Blake said.

"I understand, but I've been looking after Joe. He shouldn't be living alone. I can't even imagine how he manages during the winter. I brought him to Westcliffe this morning, thought he'd get a kick out of the events, but it was too much for him. I had to take him home."

"What did you expect? He's not used to being around people."

Amber disregarded the comment and forged on, "He showed me his family's cemetery. All his siblings died during childhood. Do you know anything about their deaths?"

"I don't know anything for a fact." Blake stiffened in his seat. "I don't talk about other people unless I have firsthand knowledge. Like I said, the Stoners were probably the unluckiest people on the planet. However, you must realize that because they were antisocial—never bothered to walk across the road to our house for conversation or anything else—we did not know much about what went on over there. Basically, just what we could see from the road." Blake delivered the explanation as if he were a professor giving a lecture.

Amber nodded, "At this point, hearsay is better than nothing. I found some skimpy entries in a journal made by Joe's mother that cast some light on her background. She didn't record any dates, but what I read was from the early years of her marriage. Your parents must have had something to say about the Stoners. They lived so close all those years. Or how about other people in the community?" Amber probed. "I'm really trying to help Joe. Please tell me anything you have heard, especially about his sister Sarah. And why was Joe the only child to grow into adulthood?"

Blake shifted his weight and stood up. Amber's hopes drained. She gave him a pleading look. Blake sighed and sat down.

"You'll pester me like a thorn, more persistent and irritating than a mosquito. I don't know much. Why can't you accept that?" Blake said.

Because, I don't believe it, Amber thought.

After a long pause, Blake said, "The Stoners had a bunch of kids, eight or ten—don't know any of their names except Joe and Sarah. The kids would have been my dad's generation, and they never went to school. Their mother was educated and taught them at home."

"Joe told me that much and showed me all his mom's books. She had an impressive collection, brought most of them with her from Scotland."

"The family was considered strange and kept to themselves. My grandmother took pity on Joe's mom. Would buy her a book now and then and sneak it to her. As soon as the old man left the ranch, my grandmother and Joe's mother would meet. I'm not sure where—but somewhere out of sight of either family. If Mrs. Stoner shared anything personal, it wasn't related to me." Blake crossed his arms over his chest.

Amber interpreted that to mean he had more to say. "What a contrast. Some people in the community go out of their way to not be involved, and others bring new meaning to the word *meddling.* I have observed both ends of the spectrum here. Maybe extremes are easier to spot in small towns."

Blake frowned as if he were confused by Amber's assessment and said, "My father firmly believed that weak minds talk about people—strong minds talk about ideas."

"Wise man. I would like to have met him," Amber said with sincerity. "Ideas are hard to come by when living in isolation. Connecting with a bigger world would have been difficult in Joe's childhood, but today, there is no excuse for small, idle minds like…" Amber let the words drift away.

"I'm not sure what you are getting at," Blake said.

"Never mind. I don't care to become one of them. You have explained the source of the new books that showed up now and then. Joe didn't know where they came from. Your father sounds like he was a perceptive person."

The compliment brought a slight smile to Blake. "I'll tell you what, my dad's opinion was, not fact, mind you, just his own personal opinion. Then leave me alone. Old man Stoner didn't allow his family to socialize. The only contact with other people was when someone needed repairs. He was strict. If he would have seen or heard that someone gave his wife a book, he probably would have burned it."

"Why was he so mean? I could really get upset about that if I let myself," Amber fumed.

"His parents were both known to be mean and controlling, you might say. Guess it ran in the family."

"All the children died in childhood. How can that be?"

"Don't know. They never went to the doctor. Joe's father delivered all the babies at home. I'm sure none of them had a birth or death certificate."

"Oh, how horrible. That makes me suspicious. A sweet child is born, lives, and dies, and the outside world never knows. I find that so sad." Amber batted her eyelids to wipe away a tear.

"Life was tough back then. People did what they had to do. Probably not right by today's standards, but you can't judge them by the whims of our current soft world. You wouldn't begin to understand what life was like back then."

Amber shot back, "I don't pretend to know. I haven't lived any of this. I just want to help Joe. I want him to be happy the last days of his life because I think he has been tormented by whatever happened to Sarah."

"My dad felt the Stoners weren't doing right by their kids, by limiting their access to the world, but back then, you didn't tell another man how to run his family."

The two children finished their ice cream cones and hopped off the bench. They yelled across the park, "Thanks for the ice cream, Mr. Hunter." And they raced down the street.

Amber shook her head. *Have I heard right?* Blake waved to the kids and acted as if this was commonplace for him. "The Stoners were a strange bunch, and no one bothered with them."

"As I mentioned, I found some notes left by Joe's mother about herself and some of the children. They are pretty sketchy and only cover the earlier years. Do you want to know what she wrote?"

"Not really. Unless it will change my life in some way—I have no need to know."

Taken aback by Blake's disinterest, Amber changed the subject. "Well, I have one other mystery on my hands. Brutus and I hike to the back part of Joe's property everyday. After crossing a large meadow, we climb an outcropping of rock formations. On the backside of those rocks is a smaller meadow where a steel building has been erected. I think that is Joe's property. Why would he have a building way back there?"

Blake's hands gripped the bench seat, and he looked like he was ready to explode.

"I know where Joe's property ends. It goes past that outcropping about a mile. I used to hunt back there on the neighboring property. Never saw any kind of structure back there. But I haven't been there for a couple of years. Who knows what Joe has been up to? It's his property. He can do what he wants."

Blake's stone-cold persona was beginning to bug Amber. It was time to move on.

"Right, doesn't necessarily mean there is a problem. It just seemed like an odd place for a building so far back on his property. I don't think he can even get to it. Well, I guess he could drive his pickup. A couple of guys come and go from it, but I have never seen Joe there."

"You probably shouldn't go nose poking around. Best you leave local matters alone and take care of your own business."

Amber knew no good would come from mention of the encounter with the motorcycle. It would only drive Blake's head deeper into the sand. Amber was miffed by how one man's mind could be so set and tried redirecting the conversation by making a small confession.

"I'll admit I'm dealing with a soap opera of my own, but my idiosyncrasies aren't even in the same league as the Stoner peculiarities. The lack of resources available to those poor children just breaks my heart."

Blake shifted his weight forward. "Again, I say, worry about your own problems. Don't interfere in others. Don't go looking for trouble."

Blake's sudden rudeness and blunt advice spoiled the newfound camaraderie. "Well, ah, thank you. This helps me understand Joe a bit more."

Blake stood and leaned into her face. "You can't help him. He's beyond help."

Blake jaywalked across the street, leaving Amber speechless. She should have expected their conversation would end on a sour note. Disappointed that Blake would never be of the same mind as she, her ego deflated. He showed no appreciation for the good she was trying to do. In fact, he mocked it. But knowing that she had bugged him made her giddy. None of the information from Blake was anything more than what she had already suspected. As she mulled it over, she became antsy. She enjoyed people watching for a short time and then checked her watch. She had enough time to stroll to the stands before the start of the rodeo.

Watching the rodeo was a great mental release, although some of the events were too much for Amber to handle. She experienced sympathy pains every time a cowboy got bucked off a horse. Even more painful was getting stomped on by the same horse. Amber stayed in the moment and banished every other stray thought from her mind. She missed the point of steer wrestling. She forced herself to stay until the end—but did keep her eyes closed during some of the bull riding. It was her first rodeo and would be her last. She much preferred the symphony.

Dried out and tired from the day in the sun, Amber retrieved her picture at the gallery and returned to where she had parked the Jag on a side street. As she rounded the corner, her car came into view. Some guy was looking it over. It happened often enough that she had grown accustomed to it. She kept walking toward the car. The guy looked in her direction, turned quickly, and dashed down the street. She was not able to see his face, but then she heard the sound of the phantom whistler.

NINE

Since Amber's plan to live as a recluse had fallen apart on day one, reading had served as her refuge from the past and the present. Some books devised the escape route from reality by entertainment and happy endings; others whisked her into plights that painted an even bleaker picture than the ones her mind had conjured up for herself. The crafted words had dragged her mind to a safe place where there was no room for worry or anticipation, a refuge from the "might have been" and the "should have been." All had disconnected her from the real world and dispensed therapy during the slow and painful healing process.

The newfound books at Joe's augmented the hoard in her cabin, but she had yet to make a trip to the Westcliffe library. The day was forecasted to be windy, which was a good reason to skip hiking and head into town. Amber planned to research the history of Westcliffe and search for information on the Stoners. Since Brutus had accepted his tether and tolerated being chained to the porch for short periods of time, she figured he would spend most of the time napping in the shade.

When Amber parked in front of the library on Main Street; her car was the only vehicle in sight. Inside the library, she found an identical situation. Other than the library assistant, Amber had the place to herself. She selected three books and sat at a carrel in the reference section. The musty smell of the older books was redolent of her grandma's attic, where wooden bellowed trunks of old clothes and papers held their secrets. A book was open in her hand, and her eyes followed the words, but her mind was far away recalling the childhood days of playing at her grandma's. Reminiscence of being young, living for the moment, and free from burdens shot a pang of regret into her heart.

She turned her attention to the book and read that Westcliffe was established as a result of silver and gold being found in the area. The railroads laid track on which to transport the riches and small towns sprang up at the end of the lines to accommodate the many miners that followed. As the gold and silver finds dwindled, ranching took over. This required more agriculture, which changed the ecology—demanding more of the land. Settlers became cattlemen and brought large herds of cattle into the valley. And ranching life was hard.

Amber sympathized with Joe's mother who she felt could attest to that dichotomy. She came to this place for its beauty, which had to equate to opportunity, and was beat down by its harshness and isolation. Only those born to be stubborn and independent survived and were happy.

Blake was the prime example in the valley. But realistically, these were necessary characteristics. Many came; few stayed. The same was true with towns. They sprouted like weeds in a garden near gold and silver discoveries and just as quickly, withered when the veins ran out.

Amber paged through another book. She read a passage and was deep in thought when voices awakened her senses. It was a conversation in hushed tones that ratcheted up with each exchange and escalated into what sounded like an argument. The speech was at that annoying ear-straining decibel—too soft to make out yet to loud to ignore. Amber tipped her head in the direction of the sound and deciphered part of the dialogue.

"This scheme was supposed to be a quick, harmless way of earning some money so we could buy a small ranch in Wyoming and be far from the influence and frustration of my parents. I'm so worried something will go wrong. I'll be glad when you can break away from your partner," a female voice said.

"Don't try to act so naive. You know big money can't be made in short order without risk. I'm nothing more than a messenger," a male voice said.

"What do you really know about these other guys?"

"You know as much as I do. I don't want to know anymore than I have to. I just want my commission for a few more weeks, and then we're out of here."

Amber looked up from the book. A young man in a baseball cap and dust-crusted jeans was leaning on the front desk, debating the issue with the young woman, who, Amber presumed, was a library assistant. They caught her gaze and immediately stopped talking.

Amber faked reading. At the *thump* of a heavy boot on the bare floor approached, she looked up.

Stiff postured, the man stood next to her table and said, "Hi, sorry we disturbed you."

The guy had long, thin legs, wore a black T-shirt, and his arms were layered in tan. His sandy-colored hair reminded Amber of a beach boy without the laid-back mannerisms.

"Oh, no," Amber said, "you didn't bother me. My mind is wandering all over the place this morning."

"Since we are staying with my in-laws, we don't have much privacy or opportunity to discuss personal matters," the guy explained.

"No need to explain. My attention span is about at the level of a six-year-old this morning. Staying interested in a history book is a test of my will."

The girl forced a smile, looked away, and offered nothing.

"We'll be quieter," the guy promised as he backtracked to the front desk.

Amber returned to her book and refrained from looking or listening. She had come with a purpose and focusing would be the only way to salvage her objective. A wasted trip into town would ruin the day for her. She jotted notes for several hours. As she closed the last book, she realized the guy was gone. She stood, stretched the kinks out of her muscles, and returned the books to their proper place. In passing, she mouthed good-bye to the girl, even though the library remained void of patrons.

Amber crossed the street to make her customary stop at the post office. After the rudeness toward her and Joe, she felt no need to play nice with Vera and her cronies. The less time spent in their presence, the better. She went to her mailbox and removed the contents. She avoided eye contact with Vera but offered a generic "hello," since the two of them were the only ones on the premises.

"Amber, how's everything?"

"Great," Amber answered and headed for the door.

"Is anything new? How's Joe? He sure looked spiffy. You must know him pretty well by now."

Amber pulled the door open. "I'm in a hurry." And she walked outside.

An internal voice prompted her to let it go. No good would come from putting Vera in her place. Like it or not, Vera and her gossip were influential around town. Amber just could not let it go.

Amber spun on her heels and burst back through the post office door. "Vera, I want you to understand that I'm just trying to help an old man, trying to give him one happy day in a lifetime filled with one conflict after another. If you can't see that, you have a problem and are the one who really needs help. I will bring Joe into town again, and I don't care what you think."

Amber was out of words. She summoned the power to stomp out the door. She walked to the corner and waited for an oncoming car to pass. The car turned out to be Ryan's pickup. He stopped at the intersection, rolled down the passenger window, and said, "Hi, Amber. What's up?"

"Well, there is something I would like to talk to you about."

The door swung open and Ryan said, "Hop in."

Amber, dressed in pressed slacks and a rose-colored lace top that brought out the natural pink glow of her skin, grabbed the armrest and pulled her body into the cab. Ryan steered his truck into the parking space beside her Jaguar and cut the ignition.

"The dreaded trip to the post office," he joked. "Did Vera have much to say? Boy, that's a stupid question, or some form of oxymoron. Let me rephrase. Did Vera have anything meaningful to say?"

"You won't believe this, but I actually left her speechless. Try to picture that!" Amber boasted.

They both tossed their heads back and laughed. Comic relief snuffed out the anger still burning in her gut. "I probably made a fool of myself and handed Vera's circle more fodder."

Ryan's eyes flew wide open. "How did you do that? No one has ever had the last word with Vera."

"Let's just say our conversation was brief and leave it at that."

"It's impossible to avoid Vera. She's been known to come around the counter and get in people's faces. Is there a problem?"

"Well, it's reassuring to know that I'm not the only person Vera picks on, but I'm not proud of losing control. She seems to bring out the worst in me," Amber hesitated. "I don't want to talk about it. I mean I have a problem with self-righteous people who are so out of touch with who they really are. Never mind. It's not what I want to talk to you about anyway."

Amber replayed each episode at the steel building, giving Ryan every detail she could remember. She could describe the build of the men, and based on their physiques and agility, she figured they were around twenty-five. The motorcyclist never removed his helmet outside the building, and the pickup driver wore a baseball cap. One was taller than the other. When she had peeked in the building, the taller guy had his back to her as he stood on the side of the ramp, guiding the cycle down. The shorter one was in the bed of the truck, balancing the backend of the bike down the ramp. He had a round face and dark hair.

"I'm sure Joe knows nothing about the building or these guys. Something is not right. Do you have any idea what any of it means?" Amber asked.

Ryan shook his head. "No, haven't heard anything around town."

"Could you investigate?"

"I could go there, but what are the chances of finding them there?"

"They don't come on any particular day or time, but they do come several times a week. I'm telling you it must be some kind of chop shop," Amber insisted.

"Maybe you should stay away from the steel building."

"Maybe I should call you the next time I see them there."

Ryan sighed. "Okay, we can give it a try."

His lack of concern and reluctance made Amber squirm in her seat. She fell silent while she debated whether to continue or if it would be better to talk to Sheriff Gavin. That was silly. Ryan was her friend, and she believed he knew how to do his job. She bit her lip and stared out the dashboard.

"Is that it?" Ryan asked, as if he were now in a hurry.

"No, I overheard something this morning in the library that might be related."

Amber told Ryan about the couple and the tit for tat they had. She asked, "Do you know them?"

Ryan's right hand had been draped over the steering wheel. Now, his fingers were tapping on the wheel, and his head turned to the outside.

A seeming eternity passed. Amber did not understand his reaction. Finally, she spoke his name. He turned his head from the outside to stare straight ahead. Even from the side view, Amber could see that his face was flushed.

"Ryan," she asked again, "do you know this couple?"

"I think I might."

"Well, who are they?"

Ryan looked at her, and her heart broke for him. "Ryan, you look like someone just died. What's the matter?"

"Just let me worry about this. Find another place to hike and try not to cause a disaster everywhere you go."

At those biting words, Amber hopped down from the truck and went to her car. When she pulled away from her parking space, Ryan still stared straight ahead.

On the drive home, even though Amber tried to push it away, Ryan's behavior laid heavy on her mind. In step with her new philosophy, Amber decided it was pointless to bring the subject up again with him. Joe appeared to be unscathed by the happenings at the steel building, as was she. She could walk away from this one.

After she arrived at the cabin, she and Brutus took Joe a chocolate chip cookie and a glass of apple juice. "Hi, Joe. I expected to see you at my cabin. Joe, are you okay?"

"Yes, just a little tired today. Can't seem to get started."

"I went to the library. I love libraries. One of these days, I will take you to the one in Westcliffe. I think you'll get as hooked as I am."

He ate and immediately fell asleep. Amber went into the library room and searched through the rest of the loose papers. She found nothing of interest.

"It's probably a waste of my time, but I'm determined to find something to help me unravel the unexplainable circumstances of Joe's life," she told Brutus.

Amber took one orange crate at a time and scoured its content. Hours went by, and she updated Brutus, "I'm looking for a pine needle in a forest."

Her back was getting weak, and she stood straight to stretch. "I'll check one more box and then give up for the day," she promised.

As she slid a book out, some papers fell to the floor. After inspecting the papers, she announced, "Brutus, get excited. This is another handmade notebook with more journal entries."

This journal was constructed of half sheets of paper bound together. Each page had one entry. Amber sat in a straight-backed wooden chair and read.

It has been four years now since I journeyed from my homeland in pursuit of a better life. Although I now have three children, I am lonely. Luke's mother loves the babies, but there isn't much to talk about. Out of nowhere, Luke's father went after me with a butcher knife, and Luke had to tie him up. There wasn't much else to do. Luke hitched up the carriage and made the long trip into Pueblo, where he committed his father to the asylum.

Luke's mother said this winter was one of the worst she had ever seen. A blizzard roared once a week, it seemed. We all were confined to the house most of the time, and I thought I would go stir-crazy. Our only saving grace was a deck of cards. Spring finally came, and we have tramped around on rock formations for hours. I feel alive again.

The institution sent word to Westcliffe that Luke's father had died. Luke went to Pueblo and brought the body home and started a family cemetery in a lovely clearing surrounded by trees on the ranch. Luke's mother sits in her rocker most of the day. Luke seems cross. I think he has trouble with all the noise and activity that five children create. Too bad, he never had any siblings.

Luke's mother didn't wake up, and Luke put her beside his father. Last month, Joseph was born. It was a difficult pregnancy because I was so heartsick over the stillbirth of Baby Stoner last year. But Joe is a joy to us all, particularly to Sarah. She has taken to be quite the little mother to him. He responds as much to her voice as he does to mine.

During the toddler ages, I didn't know if I was coming or going and fell into bed half dead every night. The older children now help with the younger ones, and life is easier for me. Poor Luke has a hard time dealing with so many under foot all the time. I have returned to reality and am teaching the older kids. I love the teaching part; wish I had more books to read.

All the children came down with a croup-type illness. The coughing was horrendous. I could hardly stand the sight of their heaving little chests. I kept them all in bed and moved from one to another day and night, applying cold compresses to their foreheads and trying to get them to take water. I did not have a full night's sleep in two weeks. Luke did not know how to help and left me alone with all of them. I am physically exhausted and spiritually broken. Little Mary drew her last breath as I rocked her the other night. She had beautiful blue eyes. Luke buried her next to Baby. Tonight, when I made the rounds trying to get a few spoonfuls of broth into their thin bodies, I was unable to awaken Mark. He had the longest eyelashes I have ever seen on a boy. I would like to be buried with him, but know I must continue for the rest of the children.

The beauty of the countryside is breathtaking, but I would be happier if we lived within a few miles of town. I would walk there and be with other people. But the ranch is far from town, and I am sure Luke would not approve of me socializing.

Amber had encountered roadblocks in her own life, but nothing that resembled a *tragedy*. She knew she could return to Denver and embrace anything that came her way. She said a short prayer asking for peace for Joe and gave thanks for her many personal blessings.

The other four children recovered and are strong. They are smart, and I enjoy teaching them. They are like little sponges, such a thirst for learning. My most satisfying moments with them are when we are in "school" each day. This is short because I'd rather teach them than read or write myself.

When I am teaching, I can forget all my disappointments. I enter a completely different world. Other times, I am cursed with headaches and must go into my dark bedroom until they pass.

The rest of the pages were blank.

Brutus and Amber poked along back to the Grants' cabin. She didn't know what else to do, so she took out pots and pans and busied her hands making chicken marsala, rice pilaf, and almond green beans. She went to Joe's and led him back to her kitchen for a dinner complete with fresh strawberries over ice cream for dessert. For the first time since they met, she offered no conversation. Her emotions were spent, and she willingly entered his silent world.

TEN

The usual call of the wild that beckoned her to the outdoors lay dormant. The question of why Melanie would make the three-hour drive from Denver to Westcliffe pressed Amber to begin her own search for answers. She poured herself a cup of coffee, heard the spring in the toaster release, and grabbed her slice of toast as it popped into a peekaboo moment. After spreading peanut butter and jam on it, she set it and the coffee on the kitchen table. Her hand rested on the back of a chair. She remained standing and took one bite of toast. While chewing, she walked to the phone. Although she had not dialed the number in months, her fingers punched in the sequence without hesitation. She verbalized a plea: "Please be there. Don't let this call go to voicemail."

Amber counted each ring and closed her eyes when the automated voice gave instructions to leave a message. She started to return the phone to its cradle. But at the sound of the beep, she spoke, "Hi, Steven. This is Amber. I hate to bother you, but something has come up and I—"

A sudden click interrupted her.

"Amber, it's great to hear your voice. I was on my way out the door to a meeting when the phone rang. Something compelled me to return to my desk and take the call. This is a pleasant surprise," Steven said.

"Oh, I'm sorry, Steven. This is a bad time. Go to your meeting. I'll call later."

"I can be a few minutes late…have a good excuse. Everyone here has lost contact with you. What are you up to? I'm sure you have found another job by now, although no one has called me as a reference."

Amber swayed in place, too hyper to sit. "Actually, I haven't tried, haven't even applied with any companies yet. I decided to take the summer off. I'm staying in a cabin in Westcliffe, communing with nature, you might say."

"Amber, this is Amber Hanson, isn't it? Communing with nature. I'm picturing some kind of hippy throwback. I can't get an image of you not shaving your legs."

Amber joined Steven in a good laugh. "No, I'm more of a mountain woman than a flower child. I went so far as to buy a pair of hiking boots. In fact, I spend most of the day time in them."

"You've become a real Calamity Jane," Steven quipped.

"Calamity is the right descriptor. Nothing has been normal, and I would love to tell you every detail, but it's a very long, convoluted story. I can almost hear your clock ticking, so I'm going to go straight to the point. Steven, you remember Melanie Carter, who was with the company for a few years? She was a goof-off and troublemaker, and I finally let her go."

"Yes, I remember she was a handful."

Amber told Steven about the anonymous thank-you notes from someone she believed had reported to her and complained to him that the sender had acquired her Westcliffe mailing address even though she had taken significant precautions against that happening. She related the discovery of a woman's body on Joe's property, which sounded creepy as she heard herself giving Steven the episode in a nutshell.

"The body has been identified as Melanie's. No one else in my personal life but you knew her. And you didn't have my address. I've no one to help me brainstorm. Have you had any contact with her, or is there any talk around the office about her? Any tidbit that might be helpful?"

Amber heard Steven inhale, and then he said "Wow" as he exhaled. "I'm shocked by all of this, including you leaving Denver for some remote and rustic site. What were you thinking? Sorry, I take that back. I'm sure you know what you're doing. It just doesn't seem like something you would do. Let me think about this and get back to you. We need to talk this through, but I really must run now. I'll find time to call you this afternoon. What's your number?"

Amber tossed her cold breakfast in the sink. What appetite she had was gone. Preoccupied by the anticipation of Steven's return call, the energy and desire to take Brutus for a romp eluded her. The nagging question of why Melanie had come to Westcliffe consumed Amber's every thought. *Melanie had no way of knowing that I'm in Westcliffe and how would she get my PO box number? Maybe she followed me out of Denver, and I wouldn't doubt that Vera would give her my address.*

Amber strolled off the deck and into the backyard. So many questions about Melanie swirled in her head. Nothing added up. Every scenario Amber played through her mind hit a dead end.

Amber walked and thought. Keeping her body moving helped churn the facts over and over in her mind. Some thoughts touched her awareness. Others hovered in her subconscious. She couldn't remember how many notes she had received. She thought one arrived after Melanie's body was found. She came to a halt at the entrance to Blake's lane.

How did I get here? she asked herself. *I was concentrating so hard, and it didn't do any good.* She sat on a boulder beside the lane, lost in thought. She bent forward and planted her elbows on her knees and held her head in her hands. Blake's white 4x4 pickup barreled down the road and swung into the lane before she could react. It stopped beside her.

Blake leaned his head out the pickup window and asked, "Is there a problem?"

"Well, no," Amber said. "I meandered as I was thinking."

"Where's your dog? Has he gotten away from you?" Blake bristled.

"No, he's chained up. I didn't intend to walk this far. I had something on my mind and ended up at your front door, so to speak."

"Hop in. Come have a cup of coffee, since you are currently free of your titanic charge."

Amber saw a smile on Blake's face, and Vera's words tumbled back to her. Blake had chiseled features, the rugged handsome look that magazine cowboys have. Seeing him happy and relaxed was a welcome change, but what caused the transformation from a grumpy middle-aged man to a neighborly gent both fascinated and perplexed Amber. One minute, he seemed angry, and the next, he was sociable.

The friendly gesture surprised Amber, and without thinking, she obeyed. She walked around the truck and climbed in. Blake drove to the back of the house and parked. They walked up a cobblestone walkway to a back door.

Amber glanced around the yard. A token grass area separated the house from a gravel pad that stretched the distance to the barn. Manicured and cheery flowerbeds decorated the foundation of the house. In a courtyard on one side of the path, a birdbath and patio furniture invited her to remain outside. Blake was holding the door open for her. She scooted through it and said, "Umm, smells wonderful in here."

"Once a week, I bake cinnamon rolls," Blake explained.

"From scratch like with yeast?" Amber joked.

"Is there any other way?"

"Yes, the kind I bake. You buy them in the frozen food section, thaw, and bake."

"I guess it's just the way I'm used to doing it. I haven't tried to find an easier way."

The kitchen was decorated in blue checks and little red hearts as seen in any country magazine. A modern pellet-burning stove positioned at an angle in a large opening between the kitchen, and the adjoining dining area added warmth even without being lit. Braided oval rugs spotted the oak plank floor stained in the same honey tone as the cabinets that lined the kitchen walls. A granny patch afghan cascaded over the back of an overstuffed plaid loveseat, and Amber could imagine the warmth and comfort it would provide if draped around her shoulders. Photos lined the walls in a hallway off the kitchen.

"Do you mind if I look at these pictures?" Amber asked as she started down the corridor. "I love the stories most pictures tell."

"I don't think most of those have much to say, but go ahead while I wash my hands and set the coffee out."

The pictures were mostly of the ranch, cattle, and horses at different periods of time. Since there were no people in the photos, it was impossible to put together any kind of tale. Amber returned to the kitchen and took a seat at a thick wood table that looked like it weighed more than her car. A gun cabinet filled with various types of shiny firearms stood guard and blended with the country decor. A paneled wall behind the loveseat held a collage of past-generation family pictures framed in various styles, ovals, rectangles, squares, circles in different woods, and antique finishes. Here were the stories if Amber had time to study the faces. None appeared to be Blake, BJ, or someone she would consider to be his wife. Those photos must be displayed elsewhere. A massive pinecone wreath adorned the opposing wall.

"Did your wife make this wreath?" Amber asked.

"Picked every pinecone from trees on the ranch. It was quite a project. But she was young and had lots of energy then."

"Your house is lovely, hope to get a tour of the rest."

Blake nodded his head and passed the plate of rolls to Amber. After an uncomfortable silence, Blake asked, "How's Joe? What are your plans for his well-being when you return to Denver?"

Amber hesitated. "Maybe the Grants can look after him."

"Haven't yet. Why would they now?"

"I haven't figured anything out yet. I have a few other things on my mind. The dead woman found in Joe's yard is a person who once worked for me. I'm totally clueless as to why she would be here."

"I wouldn't know where to start to figure that out, don't know how I could help. If you think of some way I can help, let me know. It does seem odd and probably not a coincidence," Blake said.

They chatted as they ate. Amber consumed two rolls and felt like a little pig. She was glad for the opportunity to see another side of Blake. And she gave him credit for keeping an immaculate house while running a ranch. The mansion was obscene for one person. Her silent wish for him was for BJ to return, marry, and fill the house with children. She daydreamed for a minute and envisioned it converted into an orphanage. She thought of the Stoners' small house with lots of children compared to the Hunters' huge house with only a few people living in it. *Why is the world always upside down?* she asked herself and abruptly looked at her watch.

"Oh, I need to get back. I apologize for eating and running, but I'm expecting a phone call—one I don't want to miss."

"I should get busy too. I must mend fences today. Wildlife, especially elk, run through the barbed wire. I noticed a couple of problems in one of the pastures. It's hard to keep up with everything."

As Amber hustled back to the Grants', she replayed her time with Blake. He had a way of keeping his distance. Amber figured he was skilled at building an invisible barrier between himself and others. The devices he created to protect himself, the ones he hid behind, were the very ones that kept him from moving on.

Amber's heart broke for him, and she choked back tears. Loneliness abounded in every direction around her. She realized she had allowed her circumstances to place her in the same mindset as these lonely men, hiding from the world, protecting themselves from further hurt, and making matters worse.

Ryan was right. Changes in life happen. Rather than letting them consume her, she should accept them and move on. Maybe she should have Ryan talk to Blake about getting a life, even a simple one would be better than none.

When Amber reached home, she dusted the furniture around the phone and dillydallied around the room. Joe came and napped in his wicker chair. When Steven had not called by one o'clock, she prepared lunch. She fidgeted by the phone, attempted to read and listened to music. Anxiety had her flip-flopping around like a fish washed up on shore. Steven was the only one who might be able to help. She was too edgy to read to Joe, and he left. Minutes converted to hours, and when the clock finally stuck five, she welcomed the task of making supper.

Amber slid pork chops and potatoes into the oven, made sure the sunporch door was unlocked, and went upstairs to change into some sweatpants and a shirt. Then she prepared a salad and set the table for two. She moseyed onto the sunporch to sit until dinner was cooked.

Joe sat in his favorite wicker chair, holding a book in his lap. He fumbled with it and looked at Amber.

"Did you bring a book? Is it one you want me to read to you?" Amber asked as she reached down and took the book from Joe. It was a history book on Scotland. She let the book fall open, and the musty smell permeating the pages attacked her eyes and nose.

"Boy, Joe where did you find this? It needs to sit in the sun for a few days. I'm not sure we're going to find this old history book easy reading or entertaining. It's probably going to read like an encyclopedia. But after dinner, we will give it a shot."

Amber cut Joe's meat into small pieces and prepared his plate. His appetite in the evening proved to be consistent and hearty. Amber shared her findings on Westcliffe with him and jabbered about other books she saw at the library that she thought he might like. She promised him that in a few days, she would take him and let him pick out some books to bring home.

After loading the dishwasher, Amber and Joe went to the sunporch and sat together on the loveseat. She leafed through the book in search of a chapter that might be more than facts and figures. Toward the back of the book, she found a single piece of thin parchment paper with the following entries.

> My children are all leaving me. Now, I am down to three. Rebecca was our tomboy, always trying to keep up with her brothers. She was as good a rider as they were. There is a small lake in one of the pastures in the back forty acres. None of the children know how to swim, but Becky was the most confident child I have ever known, certainly the most of this bunch. She was showing off and said she could teach herself to swim. According to Sarah, Becky jumped in the lake. The others could not help. They watched her go under. Sarah said Becky came up, slapped at the water, flailed with all her determination, but she went under and never came up again. The other children haven't eaten much or said much. It will take some time for the memory to slip to the back of their minds.

Things just keep getting worse for this family, for this lady, Amber thought. *For all of her homemaking skills, her learned knowledge, and her endurance, Joe's mother lacked the inner resources to help herself better her situation or to get herself out of her situation. She had little choice but to accept the life she was living and to allow her dreams and personal desires to die a slow death.*

Amber debated whether she should read these entries to Joe. Joe helped her out. "Please read it to me," he said.

Amber started at the beginning and read aloud. After the entry on Becky, she stopped to gauge his reaction. His expression was one of peace and relief. She read on.

Matthew was helping Luke brand cattle this spring, fell off his horse, and broke his leg. Luke had to go for the doctor. It was Dr. White's first visit to our house. He set Matthew's leg and said he would come again in six weeks. Some days later, Matthew came down with a fever and in a few short days, was gone. After Matthew left us, I stayed in my room for days. Thank God, I have Sarah. She is so capable. She just steps right in and takes my place.

I'm sure I will die soon. There isn't anything to live for. I try not to think of the past, but there is no hope for the future. In truth, hope has dimmed everyday since I stepped foot on the Stoner ranch. Luke and I had so very little in common. Yet, we tried hard to be good husband and wife to each other. I'm sorry that sadness and regret have overwhelmed me. I am not a whole person and haven't set a good example for my children on how to be anything but broken. Today, I slapped Sarah. She and Joe were hitting pebbles with a board to see how far they could bat them. I told her to get in the house and finish the ironing and that she was too old to be carrying on with such foolishness. I told her she'd really be in trouble with her father when he came home from Westcliffe. I went into my room and cried, had a headache, and needed to be in the dark. I heard Sarah tell Joe to go study. When Luke came home, Joe was in his room reading, but Sarah was not in the house. I heard Joe and Luke calling her. I made my way out of my room, the ironing sat where I had left it. We looked toward Luke's workshop, and the door was open. Joe ran to it calling Sarah and stopped in the doorway. He stood there, not responding to our questions of whether Sarah was there or not. Then he crumbled to the floor. When we got to him, his lips were blue, and his skin alabaster. Luke let out a beastly yell. Turning my attention from Joe, I saw

Sarah, there in the corner of the shop, hanging from the rafters, her neck in a roughly fashioned noose.

Amber put the papers back in the book and laid it on the coffee table. She went into the bathroom, shut the door, and cried. This was beyond heartwrenching. This bordered insanity. Vera was more right than wrong on this one. Amber splashed some cold water in her face and returned to Joe. She sat beside him and held his hand, caressing it as if it was a precious jewel. When words came, she said, "Joe, did you know this paper was in this book?"

Joe nodded.

"Then you knew what the paper says. Sometimes, you know how Sarah died, and sometimes, you remember finding her. Joe, I'm so sorry. You were just a boy. This was way more than you could possibly understand as a child. Nothing that happened was your fault. Bad things happen in our lives. It's good for you to remember Sarah because you loved her. Remember the happy times you had with her."

Nothing qualified Amber to give psychiatric advice or grief counseling. As a friend, the best she could do was recommend Joe forget the bad times and forget how Sarah died. She scoured her consolation repertoire and discovered clever Joe had been a step ahead of her. That was exactly what he had been doing.

Amber encouraged Joe to talk about his brothers and sisters, to share his memories of them with her. When her efforts fell short, she changed approaches.

"Someday, soon, Joe, I'll tell you a story from when I was a child, and then you can tell me one. It's late. Brutus and I will walk you home. I'll think of something fun to do tomorrow."

On the walk to Joe's, Amber made suggestions for the next day. They could go on a field trip, a ride in the country, or go for ice cream. Joe took his book and went into his house without voicing a preference.

It was impossible to comprehend the magnitude of the tragedies that surrounded the Stoners' lives. Amber felt numb—thinking about all those years and all those children, all the heartache and depression, all the sadness and despair. All summed up in a few entries on worthless paper. The Stoners were caught up in a private hell. The unfairness of the entire situation made Amber feel as though she had stepped into a sadistic novel. And yet, this was the sum total of one women's life.

Amber sat on the sunporch all night in a fog. By midnight, she had vowed to never look in the direction of the workshop again. Toward morning, her thoughts shifted to what she could do for Joe. And by daybreak, an idea had formulated, and Amber's agenda for the next couple of days was set.

ELEVEN

*A*mber felt that a promise, once uttered, required execution. Her heart swelled at the thought of watching Joe discover the library. Vera's verbal sting from Independence Day still burned and made Amber think twice about her plan. Allowing the busybodies to deflate her elation would be handing the triumph to the killjoys. She would rather eat bugs than grant them a victory. She devoted the morning to puttering around the house and weighed whether or not to take Joe into town. She decided giving up after only one try was adolescent.

Amber spent a few minutes playing fetch with Brutus and then buckled him to his chain tether. "Sorry, boy. I know you're not used to being tied up for long periods of time, but this afternoon belongs to Joe. I don't know how long we'll be gone. The time could go either way. Try to stay out of trouble."

She gave him a large milk bone treat to chew on and opened the car door for Joe.

"I believe I have kept every promise I ever made. It is one of my strongest convictions. I promised you an outing to the library, and that's what we are going to do. I want this to be the most elating experience of your life. You're going to be blown away by the number of books. I'm prepared to clear the way for you to enjoy this public place. Nobody better get in my face this time," she said. "We'll keep this trip simple. The library will be our only stop, and you can spend as much time as you want. We don't have a schedule."

They parked in front of the library, and Amber murmured a quick thank-you prayer when they entered and found they were the only patrons. The same girl who had been on duty during Amber's first visit was at the front desk. The girl made eye contact with Amber and smiled and continued checking in books. Amber showed Joe around every section of the library, explaining what kinds of books were in each. She pointed out fiction books were alphabetized by the authors' last names, and nonfiction titles were shelved by the Dewey decimal system. She also suggested he might enjoy the magazine section.

"The only rule you need to follow today is, if you take a book off the shelf, you must put it back in the very same spot when you're done with it. If you'd like to take a few books home with you, we can check them out, which means borrow them. Then we'll bring the books back when you are done with them."

Joe asked, "How did Westcliffe get all these books?"

"If you think this is a lot, you'd be amazed by the size of a big city's library, Joe. Libraries are one of the greatest inventions of mankind, in my opinion."

Joe wasted no time. He moved from one book to another, content to browse on his own.

Amber went to the assistant and said, "Excuse me. I have a question."

The girl arose from her station and walked to the counter.

"How does my friend get a library card?" Amber asked.

The girl handed her a brief form to fill out and a paper listing the fines, library hours, and all the regulations for checking out books. Amber started to walk away but stopped in midstep.

"I'm Amber Hanson. I hope I'm not bothering you. I'm new around here and am dog sitting for the Grants. I'm trying to familiarize myself with members of the community. I have met a few people but haven't seen you other than here. Were you born and raised in Westcliffe like most everyone else?"

The girl's face lit up. Her muted blonde hair hung straight to her collar and was held in place by a pair of sunglasses propped on top of her head. She was dressed in jeans and a striped blouse. Her long legs gave her a twiggy figure, and her youthful and flawless complexion glowed with wholesomeness and healthiness.

"I'm Rachel Archer," she answered. "I'm from here, but not everyone is. A few years ago, that may have been true, but more and more, people are moving into the valley. Some are retired and come as summer residents. Others are families trying to escape the pressures of city life. I guess they think living here would be like a step back in time and a better place for kids."

"Likely conclusion, not as many temptations or as fast a pace."

"Every problem you'd find anywhere else, you'll find here."

"I suppose that's inevitable. Technology has put us all into the same fishbowl and keeps us well connected," Amber said.

The girl laughed. "My father just preached a sermon on that very subject."

Amber speculated. More than one pastor would minister to the people of Westcliffe. The question was out before she had a chance to restrain herself.

"Oh, are you related to Ryan Tanner?"

Rachel made a slight toss of her head, and Amber was aghast at the family resemblance. "Old Ryan. Yeah, he's my brother."

Amber excused herself. "Well, it's a small world after all. I'll let you get back to work."

Of course, Ryan had family members and running into one should not dumbfound her, especially in a small town. She feared her analytical skills were being sucked out of her. She continued to grill and verbally lash herself while looking for Joe. She found him seated on a straight-backed wooden chair at a library table. She took a seat beside him. When she called his name, he jerked.

"Did I startle you, Joe? I'm sorry. What are you so engrossed in?"

Joe positioned the book between them and turned back to the first page.

"Do you know about airplanes, Joe? Has anyone told you about them?"

"No, I would like to see one," he responded and turned page after page studying each picture.

Amber explained in elementary terms how airplanes fly, how they are used, and that some are big enough to hold hundreds of passengers.

Joe's eyes doubled in size, and he asked, "People can go from one town to another through the air? I would like to ride in one."

The idea raced through Amber's head. She could take Joe on an airplane ride. She reeled herself in and let her brainstorm circulate through her mind a few times. She could hire a private plane to take Joe around the Wet Mountain Valley, but she should calculate the risks before giving Joe any false hope. One more disappointment in his life was the last thing she would want. She would consider it, and if the idea jelled, she would surprise Joe with the event. They went page by page discussing aircraft. By the last page, Joe was eager to find a different book.

Amber processed the fact that Rachel and Ryan were siblings. It pleased her that she had gleaned some information from someone other than Vera. Without her husband present, Rachel seemed relaxed and friendly, open to small talk, and unguarded in her willingness to visit with Amber.

Amber decided she should talk some more with Rachel and scanned the isles until she located her shelving books in the children's section.

"The more I think about it, the more intriguing it seems that Ryan is your brother. I've spent a small amount of time with him and certainly don't know him well. In our conversations, neither of us has talked much about our families. I'm going to give him a hard time for not mentioning having a lovely sister."

"Ry does more listening than talking until he gets to know you well." Rachel made an excuse for Ryan. Amber found the obvious affection Rachel displayed for him touching. Rachel said, "He's the oldest. I'm the youngest, and there is another brother in between. Ry was the perfect son, did everything right. He went to college, went into law enforcement. My other brother is in seminary. Nothing could make my parents happier than that."

Rachel seemed to feel incapable of competing with her brothers, so Amber offered encouragement. "It's not unusual for older siblings to set the bar high, but it looks like you have a good start. You are young yet."

"When I graduated high school last year, college was the farthest thing from my mind. I had two problems. First, I didn't like to study. I was a bit of a social butterfly all through school. And I had no idea what to study. I don't know what I want to do for the rest of my life."

Amber responded, "It takes years for many people to figure that one out."

"I was happy working in the library until I met Jackson. He is one of those not from here. He wasn't college material either. He came after high school, and Blake Hunter hired him as a ranch hand. Jackson and I met at the movies one night last summer, eloped to Las Vegas a few months later. It all happened rather fast."

"No one size fits all. There are lots of ways to begin marriage."

"My father wasn't so understanding. He thinks I'm throwing my life away. He doesn't see the potential that Jackson has, doesn't see what a hard worker Jackson is. Unfortunately, while in Vegas, Jackson racked up some gambling debt, and so, we have lived with my parents. I don't want to live at home anymore, but we're trying to pay off the debt and save money to buy a ranch in Wyoming. I need to get away from here. I have no life here."

Amber's knowledge of ranch property values was limited, but the possibility of this young couple buying a ranch anywhere seemed to be out of the question, especially on a ranch hand's salary.

"Well, what's life without dreams? I wish you well—hope you get that ranch some day."

"We're close. Jackson is partner in a motorcycle business that is doing very well."

The word *motorcycle* triggered a mental fire alarm, and Amber repeated the word.

Rachel's face lit up. "Yeah, I don't fully understand, but I think they make custom bikes for very rich guys. The money is good. Jackson says we can leave in a few months."

"Impressive. What does Ryan think of the business?" Amber asked.

"Oh, he doesn't know about it. Jackson has given up on my family and their interference. We have kept this a secret from everyone around town. I'm not sure why I'm telling you. I haven't told anyone in Westcliffe. Jackson would be really mad if he finds out I have told you. You can't tell."

"Don't worry. I won't. I have no investment here. I'll be leaving soon myself. I might know someone who would be interested in a custom bike. Maybe I could send some business to Jackson. What's the name of his business?"

"Since it wasn't a long-term venture, Jackson and his partner are just doing a few jobs. Jackson said it wasn't worth the paperwork and red tape to set up a business with all the permits and stuff. They do everything in cash and will close the shop when we leave. I don't think they are looking for new work. A few days ago, Jackson said they were going to finish what they have started and then be done."

"I suppose jumping through all those hoops would be time-consuming and tedious. Where's the shop?"

"I've never been there, but Jackson said Mr. Hunter allowed them to build a shed on his property."

"Oh, really." The disclosure caught Amber off-guard. "That's interesting and very generous of Mr. Hunter."

"Well, Ry and BJ were best friends. Jackson said Mr. Hunter allowed it because of me. Mr. Hunter couldn't show favoritism among his ranch hands, but he could make an exception for someone related to Ry."

Amber checked on Joe, who was flipping through a home improvements magazine. He looked tired.

"As soon as you're through with that magazine, we'll go, Joe. If you want to take home any books, you should pick them out."

Amber flipped through a magazine while waiting for Joe. He moved in slow motion, but she let him go at his own pace. Rather than to rush Joe, she returned to the children's area. She was studying a display of new titles when Rachel came back.

Amber did a double take. Rachel's cheery mask had changed to one of concern and worry. Rachel smiled but was mum.

"Rachel, do you know Joe?" Amber asked.

"Joe who?"

"The man with me is Joe Stoner. He has a ranch across the road from Blake Hunter and the Grants'."

"No." Rachel shrugged her shoulders. "Oh, does he live in that shack with all the junk in the yard?"

Amber nodded.

Rachel elaborated, "I've been by his place but have never seen him."

"Not familiar with the Stoners?"

Rachel shook her head. "Don't know anything. Everyone at school knew the place because it's so bizarre, but that's about it."

"Joe loves books. I thought the library would be the perfect outing for him. He doesn't get out much." Amber checked her watch. "The afternoon has slipped by. I've really enjoyed talking with you, Rachel, but we should be going. Hang in there. Things will work out," Amber encouraged. "I have one last curiosity question. Are most of Jackson's clients local?"

"I don't think so. His partner has a pickup and delivers them to other states, I think." Rachel's brows knitted, and tears collected in the corners of her eyes.

"Rachel, you look so serious and distressed. Did something happen?"

The tears turned into sobs, and Amber went to find a tissue. When she returned, they sat down at a toddler-sized fire engine red table circled by chairs; each painted in a different primary color.

"I don't think it could be any worse. Jackson just called. He didn't say where he was but said he isn't coming back, that my family should be happy now. Said something about he didn't like being given ultimatums. Too bad, my family and the law were one and the same. It doesn't make sense. I asked him what in the world he was talking about, and he said it didn't matter. This was best. I asked what's best. He said he'd be sending divorce papers, and I should sign them and move on. I'm sure he was crying when he said that."

"Oh, I'm so sorry, Rachel."

"I should have known something was wrong. Jackson hasn't been home in a couple of nights. I knew he was upset about something but thought he was staying at the Hunters'. He does that occasionally. Why would he do this? We were so close to getting a ranch and more importantly, to getting out of here."

Amber was having trouble picturing this beautiful girl in a remote area cut off from a social life. That had unhappiness written all over it, just like Joe's mother.

"I'm sorry. I don't know what to say. Do you really want to be a rancher? It's kind of a family business. Wouldn't Jackson need you to help until he was established?"

"We never talked about that," Rachel said. "I thought I would get a job in the nearest town."

Amber advised, "Give yourself some time. You need to talk with Jackson, figure out what's going on. Go home, and talk to your parents. I bet they'll be supportive and helpful."

"No, I don't want to see them. They'll think they were right."

"Then go to Ryan. He maybe knows what this is all about. And if not, at least he'd listen."

Rachel dried her eyes and blew her nose. "I have an hour until closing time. That will give me some time. Maybe I'll try calling Jackson back."

"Promise me you'll let Ryan help you sort this out. I don't want to leave you without feeling confident you have a plan."

Amber found Joe waiting at the front desk. "Do you have some books to take home?"

"No, I don't want to take any from here. I'll come here to read books."

No other words could have pleased Amber more. The library was a hit. Joe wanted to come again. Confidence charged through her veins.

"Let's go down the street and have some pizza. I bet you have never had pizza to eat before. You're going to like it."

<hr />

At the pizza restaurant, they sat at a table in front of a window overlooking the parking lot. Part of Amber was delighted for Joe, and she wanted to let herself go into a state of exhilaration, but another part of her was forlorn over the mess that ensnarled Rachel.

Caught up in the ambiance of red-checkered cloths and antiques, Amber delighted in exposing Joe to another new experience. A family on vacation occupied a nearby table and inquired about motel accommodations. The parents were engaged with three busy little bodies and paid little attention to anything else.

The waitress jabbered to Joe and Amber about the menu, as if they were passing through as well. Amber ordered a pepperoni pizza and two root beers. She and Joe had a pleasant conversation about all he had seen at the library as they waited for their pie. Once their pizza was delivered to the table, Joe spoke no more and wolfed down four slices while Amber ate one. She had the rest boxed up for his lunch the next day.

On the drive home, Amber chose some unfamiliar roads so Joe could enjoy a leisurely ride through the countryside. Perhaps she could take Joe to Denver. She could place him in an assisted living center and visit him regularly. That would work, except for the money. She lacked the nerve to ask Joe about his financial affairs out of concern that he might misunderstand her intentions. She would wait for the opportunity to present itself.

Amber switched from the future to the past. "Joe, share a childhood memory with me."

Joe turned his head toward the side window without any acknowledgement of Amber's request.

"Okay, I'll go first, " she said. "Once I walked on a fence and pretended it was a tight rope. I fell off and got the wind knocked out of me. I asked my mother if I was going to die. Of course, she laughed at me. Now it's your turn. You don't have to think hard about it. Just say whatever comes to mind."

Amber covered miles of roadway before Joe spoke. "I see my mother and Sarah standing over the kitchen table kneading bread. They made bread most every day. Some days, we had bread and milk for breakfast, lunch, and dinner."

"I know life was tough. Can you think of any fun times with your brothers and sisters?"

Joe mumbled and shook his head.

Amber wanted to say, "That's okay, Joe. If I had lived your life, I'd have selective memory too." But instead she slipped into her own reverie and let Joe do the same. For now, she was through probing Joe for information. She was leaning toward living in the moment, not the past or the future. She needed to figure out what she should do today.

Amber drove up to Joe's front door and helped him out of the car. "You should sleep well tonight, Joe, with a full tummy and lots of mental stimulation," she told him as she waited for him to enter the house. "I'll see you tomorrow." She watched until he shut the door of the house.

In the morning, Amber shook her head in disbelief. The sunporch door was open again. She had been sure Joe would fall asleep and not stir until morning. She was anxious to go hiking and rushed through breakfast. Joe was still asleep when she left some cereal and banana on his kitchen table.

She and Brutus added speed to their normal gait and reached the top of her special place in record time. She took off her backpack and settled in her nook. The time had come for discernment. She began with an exercise in silent meditation, followed by some prayer. Finally, she luxuriated in the flora and fauna and the view of the Sangre De Cristo Range. She tuned into every ray of grandeur.

"Brutus, here's some insight for you. If you want to feel the presence of the Holy Spirit, strip your view of everything man-made. A landscape void of a sight or sound of mankind brings incredible peace and brings you into a place you won't want to leave."

Brutus rubbed against Amber's leg and positioned himself as close to her as possible.

She sat in tranquility and permitted her mind to cast off all the clutter. She needed to assess Rachel's situation. From personal observation, she deduced more bikes were being disbanded than assembled. The building was not on Blake's property. The questionable partnership was conducting business in a building no one claimed to know about. The shed was far from town in a secluded area. The business was clandestine. Ryan reacted angrily when he realized there was a connection between his sister and the shed. An unregistered company operating without a license was making fast money.

"Brutus, someone put some heat on these guys, probably Ryan or his dad. But you won't believe this. I'm letting this fall to those who should be involved. I like Rachel, and I'd really like to help her. I think she's a gem yet to be discovered. I could take her to Denver, where she would find lots of opportunities to move on. But I'm staying out of it. If asked, I would enter the turbulence, but I won't volunteer. I know. This is a departure from the behavior I have displayed this summer. Believe it or not, staying out of other people's business is more my norm."

TWELVE

When Amber returned to the Grants', an older model car was parked in the driveway. "Looks like we have company, Brutus. I don't know anyone who would be making a social call, but I hope that's what it is. We have enough problems."

As she walked up the driveway, Amber spotted Rachel in one of the rocking chairs; her head bent down and cocked to one side. Brutus bounded to the porch before Amber could restrain him. Her commands of "Quiet, Brutus" and "No bark, Brutus" were more like whispers against the racket of the dog's outburst. The bedlam awoke Rachel and half the county. Dazed, she jumped to her feet, took one step backward, and fell back into the seat of the rocker. Amber corralled Brutus in her arms and told him to settle down.

Brutus ceased barking and sat down on his rump.

"I'm sorry Brutus scared you. That entire ruckus is his way of saying hello. He's overly enthusiastic when meeting new people," Amber explained.

Rachel showed little reaction and remained in the chair.

"Rachel, you look tired. Are you okay?" Amber asked.

"I didn't sleep at all last night. I spent the night in my car. I know you wanted me to go to Ryan's, but I couldn't. I can't deal with any of my family right now. They're being so unfair to Jackson."

"I know it's not easy for any of you. You feel your family is picking on Jackson. I understand. They're trying to protect you because they want you to be all you were meant to be, and they want you to be happy. They love you and don't want you to get hurt. Being torn between people who you love and who love you is a maddening position to be in."

Rachel stared at the porch floor, as if in a stupor. In the coolness of the shade, she hugged herself and sped up her rocking.

Amber chained Brutus and admonished herself for supporting the Tanner family. If Rachel had wanted a lecture, she would have gone home. Rachel had come to her because there was no complexity to their relationship. Going forward, Amber would try to keep the subject matter on the light side and only dispense advice if asked.

"I hope you don't mind, but I couldn't think of any place else to go," Rachel apologized.

"I'm delighted you're here. It's rather cool here in the shade. Let's go inside." Amber opened the door and waited for Rachel.

As if each movement was a strain, Rachel stood up and took a few steps before stumbling toward the doorway. Amber grabbed her around the waist and guided her to the sofa.

"I'm really dizzy. That's never happened before," Rachel said.

"Have you eaten breakfast or lunch?"

"No, I haven't eaten anything since yesterday. I don't think I'll ever be able to taste food again. The *thought* nauseates me."

"Well, we need to perk you up. Let's try a glass of milk and a slice of Muenster cheese to start with. You can stay for supper. Joe comes every night. He doesn't have much to say, but you'll like him. He's a very gentle man." Amber brought the food to Rachel, who took one small bite of cheese.

"Jackson isn't answering his phone. I don't know where he is. I went to Mr. Hunter's last night. I thought Jackson might be staying at the bunkhouse or at the motorcycle shop. Mr. Hunter said he hadn't seen Jackson in two days. I asked him to give me directions to the shop that he let Jackson set up on his property. He acted like he had no idea what I was talking about. I got mad. Why would he not tell me where the shop is?" Rachel said.

Amber sat beside Rachel on the sofa and offered her the cheese again. Rachel took the slice and said, "He was very short with me. He refused to help me."

Amber picked up the glass of milk from the coffee table and handed it to Rachel. "Blake is short with everyone. He tries not to get involved with people, especially if there is a problem. He's a complicated man, Rachel."

"Why would Mr. Hunter lie about the shop?"

"Rachel, Mr. Hunter isn't lying. The shed isn't on his property, nor does he know anything about it. I know where it is. I came across it while exploring Joe's property. I'll take you there tomorrow. We can sort this all out in time. Right now, you need to eat," Amber said before noticing that the plate and glass were empty.

"I'm sorry to burden you with my problems. I'm sure your life has never been this mucked up."

Amber chuckled. "Oh, girl, you have no idea how messed up my world is just now. Let me give you the condensed version. Then you'll feel better about your own situation."

Amber covered the bullet points concerning Todd, her job, and some of the shocking episodes in Westcliffe without dwelling on any of the details. They shared a good laugh over Vera's presumption that Amber and Joe were a couple. And both became melancholy over the mention of Melanie's death. Amber's objective was to show Rachel the commonalities between them.

"At least you have excitement in your life. It's not the predictable, same old, same old, same old. I find it all intriguing," the girl said.

Amber let the comment slide. Only time and maturity would help Rachel see the situation differently. By the end of Amber's story, Rachel's pallor had brightened.

"Are you feeling better?" Amber asked.

Rachel replied, "Surprisingly better."

"Would you like to take a shower while I get supper started? You can borrow some sweatpants and a shirt."

"That's probably a good idea, since I'll be in my car again tonight."

"Don't' be silly. You're not going to spend another night in your car. You can stay here unless you're too freaked out by the mysteries that surround me," Amber joked. "There's a small guest bedroom and bathroom right off this room. You should call Ryan or your parents and let them know that you are okay."

"I'll call Ry, but I'm not going to tell him where I am. I don't want him to come here and make a scene."

Amber knew Ryan well enough to suspect he would be angry with her for letting Rachel stay and for not telling him. She pushed the concern aside for the moment. One battle at a time was all she felt equipped to handle. She went to the loft and selected a gray pair of sweats and a white cotton top. "I have slim pickings in the casual clothes department."

She escorted Rachel to the guest bedroom and heard the shower running before she reached the kitchen. While the pasta boiled, she stirred up a box mix of brownies and popped them and some frozen dinner rolls into the oven.

"If you want to go upstairs to the loft bathroom, you can use my blow-dryer and anything else you need."

"I think I will. I won't be long."

Amber added carrots, broccoli, and grape tomatoes to the cool pasta and tossed it with Italian dressing. She was on the deck when Rachel rejoined her.

"You look like a new person," Amber told her. "It's amazing how a quick shower can freshen one's spirits."

"I do feel like I'm making a comeback from death," Rachel said and yawned. The sun was hovering low in the sky, sending a personal invitation to all to take a seat for its final performance of the day. Joe tottered alongside the cabin and took a seat on the deck. Amber went to the kitchen and brought out three colas and a plate of chicken breasts to be grilled. They sipped in silence—mesmerized and filled with anticipation of the climatic moment when the last ray of daylight slipped out of sight.

The three ate at the kitchen table. Rachel told them about a trip she and Jackson had made on his motorcycle to the Sand Dunes National Park and suggested Amber take Joe, although she would need to rent a jeep or ATV because the road was not passable by car.

"Well, maybe someday. The road up Mount Hermit was enough ruggedness for me for one summer," Amber said.

The dinner conversation was lively and superficial and continued while Amber cleaned up the dirty dishes. Amber unchained Brutus, and they all walked Joe home. Once he was safely inside his house, they returned to the cabin, and Brutus entered with them.

Amber lit a fire in the fireplace and shamelessly campaigned for the Denver area—emphasizing the employment and educational opportunities. "I know that's not in your plans, don't even know why I brought it up. I just love Denver and the culture there. I expect everyone to get as excited about it as I do. I would like you to visit me sometime. You and Jackson could spend a few days with me, and I could show you around."

"I'm sure there would be endless things for me to see and do, but what would you show Jackson?"

"The Denver Museum of Nature & Science is interesting if he likes dinosaurs and outer space. And the IMAX theater there is always worth the time. We could go to the gold-domed state capitol building and be photographed standing on the thirteenth step. It denotes the elevation at one mile above sea level, or maybe it says '5,280 feet'. I can't remember for sure. If he likes roller coasters and other scary rides, we could go the Elitch Gardens. I'm sure I could keep him entertained for a few days," Amber said with confidence.

They talked about the future, both avoiding dealing with the present or past. Amber popped corn, and they took turns throwing a kernel into the air for Brutus to catch in his jumbo jaws. Brutus nudged them with his muzzle. His childlike behavior tickled Rachel. She petted him and yawned aloud.

"Before you fall asleep, you must call Ryan," Amber reminded.

"I warn you, it's going to be a very short call."

Rachel told her brother she was fine and was staying with a friend and hung up before he had time to say anything.

Although Amber had hoped for more, it was at least a first step. Rachel was fading fast and went to her bedroom. Brutus stretched out by the fireplace, and Amber went to the loft and read for several hours.

In the morning, both Brutus and Rachel were well rested and energetic. Amber had tossed and turned most of the night and felt like she had lead in her feet as she made breakfast. After eating, they headed out to the rock formation. They stopped at Joe's and dropped off some cereal and yogurt.

"Joe doesn't get up this early. He is a night wanderer," Amber explained.

Rachel looked puzzled. "How can he wander around at night? He seems to have trouble walking during the day?"

"I can't explain it Rachel. It's a mystery."

Amber showed Rachel the points of interest along the way and tensed up as they motored by the workshop. She sighed a prayer of thankfulness when Rachel did not inquire about it. She showed Rachel the Stoner family cemetery where the birds played a serenade. The sunshine warmed Amber's shoulders, and the world seemed right. They climbed to the top of the formation and reached Amber's favorite spot and lounged in the splendor of the setting.

"I can't believe how beautiful this area is. I didn't know it even existed," Rachel said.

"I agree. This has got to be some of the most majestic scenery in the area—in all of Colorado in fact." But as Amber looked around with pride pumped up like a new parent, the day felt different to her. She reasoned it was different. No one had ever been with her to her rock before. She had made the venture on Rachel's behalf and eliminated her usual routine by leaving her backpack at home. She felt lost without it, but the plan was to go there and then straight back, no reflecting or meditating. The circumstances were different.

She tried shaking the feeling that lurked like a sixth sense, like a sneeze that refuses to come but won't go away. Standing on top, the world was perfect. Everything was in place, and the cloudless sky was the most beautiful yet. As she longed for time to stop, her premonition revealed itself. She sensed her visits to the rock would end before she was ready to abandon them.

Time stood still as they took in the splendor of the setting, and Amber delayed the inevitable as long as possible. When Rachel stirred, Amber turned toward the shed and spoke, "I think this is Jackson's shed."

Rachel turned to look and sprang into motion so fast that Brutus jumped into attack position. The door to the shed was open, and the black Harley was parked in front. Rachel skipped down off the formation and sprinted to the shed before Amber had made it to the bottom. Amber was almost to the shed when the bumblebee-yellow pickup roared out from inside the shed and thundered off. The driver never looked her way. As she reached the shed, Rachel and Jackson came out.

Jackson was buckling his helmet and shot Amber a look that could kill. He flung his leg over the bike and jumped on the starter. Rachel briefly looked at Amber and hopped on the back of the bike. The customized mufflers were deafening, and the cycle was out of sight before Amber gathered her wits. She remained planted and tried to digest what just happened.

"Oh, Brutus, things just keep getting worse," Amber said. "Well, here's our chance to go inside."

Amber squinted while her eyes adjusted to the darkness. She walked from one end of the shed to the other. It was empty, not even a screw had been left behind.

She climbed up the formation and dawdled on the top. No need to hurry to the next predicament. She sat in her spot and meditated. If ever she needed to clear her mind, now was the time. Somehow, her mind made a big leap from Rachel to Steven Kern. He had not returned her call and that tormented her. He had never been rude before. It was possible that he forgot, but not likely. Perhaps he didn't want to get involved. That was hard to believe. He had said he was clueless. Maybe he had nothing to say. She'd better leave the issue alone.

Amber tarried home, stalling at every opportunity. That sixth sense nagged her and warned her that she was about to walk into some kind of flytrap.

When she was in sight of the cabin, she could see that Rachel's car was gone. She had suspected it would be. "Now comes the hard part, Brutus. I must call Ryan. I don't think he's going to be very pleased with me."

Brutus barked at her and followed her into the cabin. Part of Amber yearned to yell across the county, "Run, Rachel, run. Free yourself." Another part wanted to cry out and warn Rachel that she was running from one form of captivity to another.

~~~~~

The call to Ryan was tense. He was impersonal and short on words. He chewed Amber out for harboring a runaway, and Amber defended both herself and Rachel. "She's not a criminal,

Ryan. She's just a kid in over her head. She needs your support, not your lectures."

Continuing would have been an exercise in futility. Ryan was silent on the other end of the line. "What will happen to Jackson?" Amber asked.

Ryan wouldn't answer. "Come on, Ryan. You can work through this. If you don't answer this one question, you mustn't like me very much. Just tell me what Jackson is facing."

After a long pause, Ryan said, "It's up to him."

Before Amber could continue the conversation, she heard the disconnect click of the phone.

THIRTEEN

A mber tossed and turned; dozed on and off. Brutus's bark brought her to an upright position. She sat motionless in the middle of the bed and listened. Brutus growled and then went silent. She slipped out of bed and went to the window where she squinted in search of light. From the upstairs window, she looked down on the landscape where a splinter of moonlight cast a silvery beam on the yard. A shadow scuttled across her line of sight. Her heart skipped a beat and then raced. Someone was out there. The question paralyzed her and held her at the window, frozen in time in her white cotton nightgown. The house was silent. Brutus was silent. The world was silent, and silence was good. *Oh, that Joe is out there roaming like some nocturnal animal, but he needs to realize that his survival instincts are fading fast,* she told herself and headed downstairs.

After verifying that the sunporch door was locked, she bundled herself in a fleece throw and reclined on the sofa to read a magazine and listened to Chopin on her portable compact disc player. Slumber seeped in, and her eyes drifted shut. The uninterrupted night of deep sleep was long overdue. The dim light of dawn outlined her unchanged form on the sofa. She flipped onto her back and brought the gray ceiling into focus. Her eyes closed, and she bordered a dream state. After a number of false starts, she sat up and stretched her arms.

She stood and went to the sunporch to capture the essence of the Sangre de Cristo Mountains during their rebirth from darkness. Telltale shadows littered the room and created spooky figures meant to frighten. All this paled in comparison to her teeth chattering at the sight of the open porch door.

As so many times before, she shut and locked it and willed her mind to think of something else. While in the shower, she berated Steven Kern for not returning her call and belabored the fact that everyone was unreliable these days.

As they ventured out, Amber saw Blake in the hay field on a tractor. He had been in the field for days, cutting and raking hay. Amber and Brutus roamed most of the afternoon and rendezvoused at their favorite spot.

"I don't know why I had such eerie feeling when I was here with Rachel. I guess I'm being selfish. I don't want to share it with any other humans. Everything seems right today," Amber told Brutus before he scuttled behind a rock out of her sight. She focused on reading, uninhibited by time. A shadow fell over her book, and she speed-read to the end of the chapter. She gathered her gear and stuffed it into her backpack as the sky began a ballet performance. One by one, thunderhead clouds formed and in a matter of minutes had filled the sky. Their pure whiteness turned to gray and then black. Their movements shifted from adagio to allegro without skipping a beat. As the sky darkened, the clouds began to tumble over each other, as if they were in an atmospheric clothes dryer.

"I'll race you to shelter," Amber challenged Brutus.

They hustled until they reached the cemetery. From there, they ran, driven by fear and unease. Something just did not feel right. They simultaneously stepped onto the front porch when lightning sliced through the clouds in a fireworks display, and thunder broke the sound barrier. Amber watched from the sunporch, and Brutus hovered as close as possible by her side. The electrical component of the storm ceased and hail encased them in a white chamber. She stepped away from the windows and covered her ears with her hands to deaden the deafening noise. The sound stopped, as if she had turned off a radio. Brutus still whimpered. Although the storm's duration was short, it left a mess in its wake. Three inches of pea-sized hail cloaked the vista. Amber put on her hiking boots and went outside to assess the damage. It was a huge relief that there were no broken windows or dents in the siding of the cabin. Flowers in the beds around the cabin were shredded, but their stalks stood straight. She examined the Jag and confirmed what she expected. Little dimples were spread across the hood, top, and trunk of the car. The side panels were untouched.

"Good news, Brutus, the hail came straight down. It would have been a lot worse if there had been wind with it. The dents are small. The bad news is they will need to be fixed. There goes a deductible payment."

Slipping and sliding around the yard, Brutus tried to find a way to balance on the slick surface. His failure egged him on to keep trying. When he grew tired of falling down, he discovered he could eat the hail and plopped down to feast. Freshness wept from the icy air and Amber found herself trapped between the trauma of the force of nature and the revival of a sunny, calm day. The sun burst through the grayness and wiped away the mistiness in one big swoop.

Blake drove down the road and stopped at the driveway. "Is everything okay?" he yelled from his truck.

Amber skated to him. "Jag got pelted, but no major damage to the cabin. How about you?"

"Well, I will have to rake that field again, and the hay is now worth half as much to me or anyone else. My clover and timothy hay usually bring the highest prices, but thanks to Mother Nature, some of the nutritional value has been lost. But that's ranching in Colorado."

"I see how your work is never done," Amber said. As Blake drove off, she sent mental kudos to him for his ability to be pragmatic yet not discouraged. "I think that man has nerves of steel, Brutus. I guess it goes with the territory."

Amber chained her sidekick and commissioned him to guard the cabin. She left her hiking boots on the porch and entered the welcome sanctity of the cabin. While reading, she heard a thump on the front porch that gave her a start. She berated herself for being so easily spooked, opened the front door, and forced herself to step outside. Her world was completely still, and she felt as if she were the only creature on the planet. She took another step and tripped over her boots.

"Oh Brutus, why are you messing with my shoes?" Amber asked.

The thunderstorm did more than knock nitrogen out of the air, which turned the countryside the brightest green possible. But it also washed away two nuisances. After that afternoon, no more open porch doors and no more whistling. Uneventful daily living became the norm for the next few weeks.

The solitude and routine lapsed into mundane. She had accomplished her mission of disconnecting herself from Denver and all those related to it and had reached a desire to move on. The need to confide in someone who understood her journey ran rampant. Amber had walked for miles with Brutus, looked after Joe, and found nothing more to occupy herself.

She sat on one leg as she dialed the number connecting her to Olivia. She began the conversation with an apology for the belated call and went right into a report on the storm: "The Jag's going to need a little bodywork."

"You must be devastated. You take such good care of your stuff. Are you counting the days until you can get it repaired?" Olivia asked.

Amber's answer disclosed an attitude that seemed foreign even to her. "Not, really. When I put the situation in perspective, I realize it's not a big deal. It is what it is, and it's fixable. I can honestly say a car is not a big deal compared to a rancher's livelihood."

Amber recapped her two positive adventures with Ryan.

Olivia interrupted before Amber told her about the chop shop. "Sounds serious."

"We're just spending some time together. He's officially dating someone. In fact, I met her. When she gave me her hand, I couldn't tell if I was supposed to kiss it or shake it. She thinks she's royalty, handshakes like a wet noodle. But they actually make a nice-looking couple. Besides, he's too young for me."

"You're only thirty-five. How much younger can he be?"

"Probably five or six years."

Olivia balked, "That's nothing. Don't dismiss possibilities."

"Does it sound like I belong here? Besides, Ryan and I are too opposite."

Olivia chuckled, "Well, that's not a bad thing. You know what they say. Opposites—"

"Yes, I know. Opposites *attract*, but I also know they make each other miserable over time. It's hard to maintain a long-term relationship when you're at odds with each other over most everything."

"Why don't you bring Ryan to LoDo for a long weekend? Maybe you have more in common than you think."

"If you knew Ryan, you'd realize how preposterous that would be. The bottom line is Todd was low maintenance. Ryan is high. He's always on the move and making things happen. He reminds me of a toddler, always into something but is not good at cleaning up after himself. He gets excited in a laid back way. It's a frustrating combination. He could get excited about burnt toast. Even though my meetings with Gavin, the sheriff, were brief, I'd say he shows more possibilities than anyone else in Westcliffe. But I don't think he'll be stopping by for a social call. He keeps a low profile. His name doesn't come up around town. I've been spending most of my time with my good buddy."

"Who's that? Joe?" Olivia asked.

"No. Brutus, of course. Joe's a worry. Brutus has become a great companion."

"I can't believe you are getting attached to a dog. You're one desperate woman." Olivia sounded more astonished.

Amber considered the comment and in self-defense, said, "Don't be nasty. Desperate is an overstatement. It's all part of my changing perspective. Brutus is more like a person than I could've imagined. I talk to him a lot, and he never disagrees. Switching subjects. I can't believe the middle of August is here. My time here is almost over. So far, I've only told you the good news about my adventures with Ryan.

"The melodrama does somewhat continue in a couple different ways. During our horseback ride, we came across an abandoned car. This is beyond my comprehension. That twilight zone you were so sure I had entered—resurfaced. The car belonged to the dead person, and she has been identified as Melanie Carter. You might remember her. She worked for me about the same time you left the company. In fact, I had to fire her, and I'm sure she had been sending me the notes."

"What, who? Are you sure? Oh, that can't be. I don't believe it."

"Calm down, Olivia. There's nothing to get so upset about. I have no idea why she was here. I'm sure the sheriff considered me a person of interest, but he has nothing to tie me to the murder. My days have been quite ordinary lately. I feel really good."

"I need to go, Amber. I'll talk to you later."

And the phone went dead.

FOURTEEN

mber awoke, showered, and blow-dried her hair. She bounced down the stairs with an extra spring in her step. In two weeks, the Grants would be home, and she was psyched about starting anew in Denver.

On her many walks with Brutus, she had worked through her breakup with Todd. She hated admitting that her mother was right. Amber hoped to balance work time and leisure time more proportionately in the future. The day after day of solitude with Brutus as her companion and looking after Joe had brought peace. Contrary to what she believed her disposition to be, she found satisfaction in caring for both of them. Understanding the circumstances around Sarah's death and the trauma it caused a young Joe brought Amber closer to him. Her concern added a new dimension to their relationship.

Several times, she had taken Joe to the library for the afternoon. Rachel was gone. Her replacement was an older woman out of Vera's gang. Their conversations were limited to hellos and goodbyes. Neither made any effort to engage the other.

"Joe, I think I have figured out how to survive around here. Keep a low profile. You and Blake and Gavin Rivers live that reality. And Ryan seems to have disappeared. I'm sure as soon as my Jag hits the city limits, he runs for cover. I know he's out there. Rachel must be in hiding as well. I hadn't pegged Ryan as someone to hold a grudge. That's why you and I and Brutus get along so well. What we see is what we get," Amber said.

Joe had the eagerness and delight of a child going into a toy store. During each trip, Amber stopped at the grocery store and bought conveniently prepared food, fresh fruit and veggies, and baked goods for Joe to have. His face had filled. A dimple had sprouted on his right cheek.

She had chosen today as Joe's birthday and had planned to surprise him with a birthday cake. She had searched the library and county court house records for a birth record but came up empty. Blake had that right. There were no birth or death certificates for any of the Stoner children. When in doubt, pick a date—any date. She got up before the dampness of the night burned off to bake and ice a cake. Now, she and Brutus would gather some columbines to artistically place around the blue letters that spelled "Happy Birthday, Joe."

Amber went to the front porch, expecting the inevitable attack from the playful canine. She listened for the usual therapeutic twittering of the birds and felt an eerie chill that all was too quiet.

Brutus's chain was still anchored on the porch post, but its end was abandoned in the flowerbed. The dog's unbuckled collar hung at the end of the chain. She scouted the horizon, anticipating the scamp to come loping out of nowhere. Amber called and called his name. *Nothing.* Every sensor in her body reacted to combat the fright that welled up inside her. She raced to Joe's house and burst through his door. Joe sat on the sofa, his hair was disheveled, and his feet were bare.

"Did you unbuckle Brutus's collar Joe?" she asked. "Brutus's gone. I need to find him. Have you seen him?"

"No," he answered in monotone. Although his answer lacked conviction, Amber could tell he had not been outside yet that morning.

Amber returned to her cabin and picked the Jag keys up off the kitchen counter. She checked the sunporch only to find the door wide open once again. She swallowed the golf ball–sized lump in her throat and heard the jingle of the keys in her own trembling hand. After a long absence, the door-opening phantom was up to his old tricks again. She could no longer believe Joe was responsible.

Amber searched the roadways in the vicinity of the cabin, stopping every quarter of a mile to yell for Brutus. Nothing. She hollered until her voice lost its volume. She pulled up to Blake's house. A porch swing swayed in the breeze and beckoned her to sit and zone out. Instead, she stomped to the front door. She knocked, huffed, knocked again, and waited. Determined that Blake must be home and must answer her questions, she took one step closer to the door and rapped until her knuckles were red. The sound of a heavy booted step hammered against a wood floor. Blake opened the oversized door, giving way to a full view of the front room; its enormousness commanded her attention. Leather sofas and chairs were clustered in conversational areas on either side of a fireplace that could heat up the great outdoors. The walls were decked with paintings of cattle ranches and mountain scenes. Blazing bronze statues of horses, deer, elk, and bears were overstated knickknacks. Everywhere her eyes went, they landed on some form of art. The Western showroom left her openmouthed.

For a moment, her disappointment in not getting a grand tour on her previous visit overshadowed her panic.

The tastefully decorated room reflected what she thought to be Blake's true personality—the one hidden beneath veneers. The room followed a different theme from the homey kitchen, and although the styles were dissimilar, they were complimentary. Obviously, this was Blake's room. The kitchen was his wife's.

"What do you need? I've an appointment in Pueblo and need to be on the road already," Blake asked.

"Oh, um, Brutus's missing. His collar is still attached to his chain. The collar has been unbuckled, and I can't find him. I've been searching for hours."

"That probably means he's out in one of my pastures, chasing my cattle," Blake accused.

Amber pleaded for sympathy and help. "He can't unbuckle his own collar. Something's not right. Did you see him at all this morning?"

"No, I've been really busy, but you better find him before he does any damage." Blake stepped onto the porch and pulled the door shut behind him. He walked past Amber and slid into the driver's seat of his shiny pickup parked in front of the house. *How can his truck not have a speck of dust on it?* she wondered. He hopped in and was out the lane before Amber had gotten into her Jag.

"That's it," she said to the taillights of Blake's truck. "I'm not a psychologist, but I'd say he either has a split personality or humongous mood swings."

Back at her cabin, Amber cast the rest of her pride to the mountaintops and called Ryan. She had missed breakfast with Joe, so she fed him brunch. Her stomach hung in her throat. She sipped on a cup of warm water while she and Joe sat in silence.

Now was the time to upgrade worry to panic. Something was wrong. She prayed a silent prayer that was a plea for protection of Brutus and for simplicity. Her time in Westcliffe had become complicated again. She prayed she would find Brutus tearing through the countryside, like greased lightning, and they would share a good laugh. All she wanted was a celebratory homecoming.

Amber paced the length of the front porch. When she saw the sheriff's SUV coming, she ran to the end of the lane. Ryan braked to a stop, and she jumped in. She updated him, "I have called and called for him. I have driven down all the roads. Brutus never misses breakfast. It's his only meal of the day. I should've brought him in last night. I usually do, but with the Grants coming home soon, I thought I'd better make him an outside dog again." Amber held back tears. This was not the time to cry.

"Let's drive off-road and start with the unoccupied land behind the Grants' property."

They zigzagged across the open fields covering every parcel she and Brutus had ever hiked. The vehicle crawled over bushes, small boulders, and low areas to high ridges. They found nothing.

Amber's thoughts momentarily shifted. Her inner voice told her to let it go, but her anger spoke louder. "I have a question for you. How can God allow so much tragedy in one family? The Stoner kids didn't have much of a chance in this world. How can God allow such atrocities against innocent children? How can a loving God allow all the evil that is in the world? How can a loving God deal with people who are in church every Sunday, but whose actions are un–Christian like?"

"You probably need to ask a professional that question, someone better versed that I am, but I'd say he delivered those kids. They're in a better place. Don't be worrying about them now. That's history. Look to the future," Ryan said.

Amber tried to tell Ryan how each Stoner child died, but the words stuck in her throat. Reliving the emotional devastation associated with each one was more that she could handle; plus, she had unfairly put Ryan on the spot.

"You're good at not getting caught up with things you can't change. I haven't mastered that yet," Amber complimented him. Ryan turned his vehicle toward the road.

"I don't think there is much else we can do to find Brutus. I don't know where else to look. We could search forever and not find him. You'll have to wait it out. I think he'll come drifting home on his own."

"You think, or you know? Either you know or you don't know. Thinking you know won't cut it. Do you know?" Amber's corporate training bubbled up and out. There was no room for error or misjudgment at this moment. "I'm not going to give up.

I'll think of something. Just take me back to the cabin. I'll do the rest myself, go it alone, as usual."

Ryan sighed, and Amber knew she had gone too far—had said words she could never take back. Words that now and forever cut an abyss between them. If she were being tested as to how low her spirits could go in one morning, she had passed with an A plus and earned bonus points. She had to fight a compelling desire to bail out of the SUV and run away.

As Ryan wheeled his SUV out of the field onto a side road, Amber's eyes locked onto an object at the side of the road: a brown bump in the distance.

"There, there," she pointed.

Before the SUV had come to a complete stop, she bounded to the ground. Her feet spun on loose gravel, and she performed a few acrobatic steps to prevent herself from falling. All the while, her motion was forward until she reached Brutus. Amber sat on the hard roadbed next to her good buddy and with unusual strength, lifted his upper torso into her lap. The circle of blood where he laid left a glossy, wet spot on the dry-packed soil.

Ryan jumped out of his sheriff's car and stood a few yards away—speechless and motionless.

At first, Amber sobbed, and then grief manifested into deeper oceans of tears. She rocked Brutus back and forth and cried deep, mournful utterances of sadness. She begged Brutus to answer, to respond, and pleaded with the dog to show a twitch of life. She sat, holding Brutus and crying until no more tears came. She heard a voice talking to her, but she did not look up; she could not take her eyes off the troublemaker who had become her best friend and did not deserve this.

At the point of emotional depletion, Amber came to her senses. "I was down this road earlier. He wasn't here. I haven't heard any gunshots this morning. Nothing adds up."

Ryan sat next to her on the ground and put his arm around her. "Let's go back to the cabin. I'll come back for Brutus."

Amber turned on Ryan in a rage. "Do you know manipulation when you see it?"

"I know what the words mean. If that is what you are asking."

"Look at Meredith, and you'll see it in action. And Blake Hunter has accomplished his mission. He shot Brutus dead. You must arrest him! I'm sick of Westcliffe."

Ryan retrieved Brutus's body. Amber changed into clean clothes and threw her blood-soaked outfit in the trash. There was no way she wanted anything in her possession that had once had Brutus's blood on it. At the moment, she had no intention of taking anything back to Denver that would remind her of Westcliffe.

She sat on the sunporch and stared out into the vacuum that surrounded her. Her mind rummaged for a safe place to hide. She attempted to bathe in the breathtaking grandeur of the panoramic mountain scene displayed before her. It repulsed her, and she turned her head away. She saw no beauty there or anywhere. She tried being numb, tried to sit quietly, and feel nothing, but angry thoughts crept into her brain. She was fed up with Todd, Steven Kern, her mom, Ryan, and especially, Blake. Letting go of the frustrating dynamics in all those relationships seemed impossible.

Clanking, scratching sounds came from the backyard. Amber moved to the deck. In the distance, Ryan was digging. He toiled over a small indentation in the ground. One thought drifted into Amber's conscience. There was much digging to be done. Brutus would require a big hole. In a death march cadence, she went to Ryan. She reached out and took the shovel from him. "I'll dig. You go make a coffin," she said.

Digging was hard, but Amber chipped at the rocky soil. She dug and dug. Some shovel loads were no more than a few spoonfuls of dirt. The removal of each particle was progress; every stone was a labor of love. Amber persevered for hours. When

Ryan returned, he brought a crowbar with him, and together, they went the distance.

As they stood looking into the hole, Amber was oblivious to the sound of boots walking in the grass. Blake appeared and asked, "What's going on?"

Amber looked away, had nothing to say. She let her shovel fall to the ground, and she walked to the cabin. Before reaching the deck, she looked over her shoulder as Ryan and Blake lowered Brutus's pine coffin into the grave.

In the cabin, Amber went to the upstairs bathroom and ran cold water over her palms. Skin from broken blisters hung loose. The clear water from the faucet turned red as it flowed from her hands to the drain. She applied antiseptic and bandages and returned to the deck as Ryan and Blake completed their task of pitching dirt into the hole until a mound formed over it.

As Ryan and Blake drove out of the field, Ryan called to her, "I'll check with you later."

Amber was alone. The grave beckoned her, and she went to it. She sat on the ground beside it and said mental good-byes to her good buddy until her emotions were spent. Now that Brutus was properly buried, she returned to the sunporch where she intended to sit until her mind and body reconnected.

A spark of fright ignited her reflexes when she realized someone other than Joe was seated in Joe's wicker chair. Her instincts screamed for her to run. Those same reflexes told her it was too late, and her disgust boiled to the top.

FIFTEEN

T he man grinned at Amber and spoke, "Surprised to see me, Amber? You don't look like your usual perky self. Did your favorite pet die today? I'm so sorry. You have my condolences. Well, not really. I think you deserve a little pain and suffering." He stood up and pulled a gun out of his pocket.

Amber felt such repulsion she feared she would be sick. This man had no business being in her cabin or in Westcliffe for that matter. When she entered the sunporch and saw him, she expected a verbal encounter. But the glint of a gun gave her little time to devise plan B. Her only strategy was to keep him talking and stall for time while she figured out what was going on in his head.

The muted click of metal stopped all action in the cabin. The sound of the twisting and turning of the front door knob was amplified by the momentary silence in the room. Whoever was on the other side struggled to force open the door. The noise stopped. Amber feared Joe was on the other side. Even though she had never believed in mental telepathy, Amber closed her eyes and tried to send a message to Joe, warning him of the danger inside the cabin. *Go home. Go hide from this lunatic in my presence.*

"Now, who could that be?" The intruder asked. He went to the door and flung it open. "Do you have ghosts around here? Who is the phantom monkeying with the door?" he said.

Amber sighed a thousand breaths of relief. "I don't know. Lots of weird things happen around here."

"Oh, I think I can explain every one of them," he taunted. "I'll be more at ease if you sit, Amber." He hurled a kitchen chair into the middle of the room, grabbed Amber by the arm, and shoved her down. She landed on the edge of the seat, almost toppling the chair.

"Better make yourself comfortable. I'm not sure how long our little chat might last," he said. He pulled a leather shoelace from his pant pocket with one hand and put the gun in the same pocket with the other hand. In one swift motion, he pulled Amber's hands to the back of the chair.

"This is absurd. You don't need to tie me up. I'll sit here as long as you like and talk about whatever you like," Amber pleaded.

"I don't think so, Amber. I'm going to preside over this meeting. And this is to insure that I have your undivided attention."

Playing the guessing game exasperated Amber. "Why are you here? How'd you find me? What do you want?"

From where she sat, she could see the entrance to Blake's ranch. She forced herself not to smile at the sight of the old foam green pickup as it poked along and maneuvered a wide turn into Blake's lane. She wondered how much sense Joe could make of the situation. He obviously understood enough to go for help. Help would arrive and the insanity would all be over soon. "Did you kill Brutus?" she asked.

He removed the pistol from his pocket, stood over her, and flashed it in her face. "The dog napping was just to heighten your distress. It was fun watching you search hour after hour. That burial ground of car parts provided an ideal vantage point for me to watch the calamity unfold. Trust me. I enjoyed every minute of it."

"You did more than take Brutus. Why? What do you want?" Amber demanded.

"It's all about power. You of all people should know that I want to see you *powerless*. I didn't come here to harm the dog. I wanted to watch you fret over him. I'd say that part of the plan worked extremely well. I admit that I got carried away with the dog. After coaxing him into my car, it was easier to kill him than deal with the beast."

Amber tried to speak the monster's name, but it stuck in her throat. The realization that anyone she knew was capable of such abnormal behavior shocked her. It was the saddest hurt she had experienced to date. She chose to stay as detached as possible from him. She feared that saying his name would emotionally build a bridge between them, one that she preferred be nonexistent. She closed her eyes in an attempt to disassociate the name from the face. If she considered him a stranger, his actions would be more tolerable because she would view him as being from a different world, a different part of society, and a fluke that their paths should meet. That was wishful thinking.

But he was part of her world, and dealing with his dark side was now on her plate. She made a snap decision that it would be better for her to establish a personal connection than to show her repulsion. As her thoughts began to gel, she pelted out his name.

"Warren, Warren, Warren. I'm blown away. I can't picture you hurting anyone. What's wrong with you? I can understand you being angry with me, but your temperament isn't mean. Killing an innocent dog is more than mean—it's evil. What has happened to you since the last time I saw you? I would never have thought you capable of being sinister. Tell me, please. What's going on?"

Warren chided, "Oh, it is quite a story, Amber. Working with you had a couple of advantages that you don't know about. That's the most luscious part. Miss Know-It-All doesn't have a clue."

"What are you talking about? You're not making sense. This is beyond reason. You've made your point. Now untie me. We'll figure out someway to deal with Brutus's death."

Amber squirmed in her seat and yanked her hands, expecting them to slip out of the laces that held her bondage. Warren had shown no mercy in the tightness, and she realized her hands were numb stubs.

"Sorry, Amber, you aren't going to be able to fix this. And I'm way beyond the dog."

"Warren, please, please. Tell me what's going on."

"I'll tell you part of it, but I'm not going to tell you all of it. You have no idea what a rush I get when I have information you don't." Warren paced back and forth in front of Amber.

"I never realized we were in a competition with each other."

"Everyone wants to take down the big shot. You've played the game. I'm sure there are a number of higher executives that you have dreamed, or even plotted, to bring down," Warren said.

There were plenty of people at work Amber had disliked for one reason or another. Wishing failure on them or manipulating them never crossed her mind. If they were unsuccessful, she was oblivious to the human emotional side and considered it their problem. She would never intentionally cause them to fail. She had focused on her own responsibilities.

Warren stopped pacing and straddled a kitchen chair he had placed close to Amber. He became a chatterbox. "I decided this would be the absolute last time I drove these blasted roads. I detest these windy, hilly roads. First, you hit the gas to go uphill and then the brakes to keep from going over the side of the road coming downhill. But I've been here enough to master the technique. It was what I had to do to bring you down, Amber.

"Every time in my life I tried to step across the finish line, some ignorant know-it-all got in the way. Someone always got in the way. This last time—it was you."

"How did I get in your way? I coached you. I spent hours trying to mentor you so you could be successful."

"I've always been picked on and ordered around by the world. We live in a place full of morons—idiots who think they know everything. I'm not dumb, Amber. I'm smart. I know lots more than anyone, especially you, gives me credit for. But what's the use? I'm tired of being inconsequential, unimportant, and unnoticed. It's payback time."

Amber knew she had to keep him talking even if it all didn't make sense. She also had to try and keep him calm. "I'm still happy to try to help, Warren, but I don't know what you want. What do you want from me?"

"I want you to know exactly what it's like to be me, and I want you to pay for what you took away from me. I've got this girlfriend now I call June Bug. You know her as someone else. She's the one that really set this in motion and encouraged me to take control. She helped me see that if I did not want to spend every Friday and Saturday night stuck in a lousy basement apartment that I had to take action."

"Warren, I really don't know what you are talking about."

"I hate my apartment, hate everything it represents. I should be living in a townhouse, or condo on a park, with flowerbeds full of color and endless walking paths through lush grass. It should be close to LoDo and downtown, near those fancy lofts that people pay millions for. I should be near the people of influence, the movers and shakers of the world."

"Is this about money? Do you need money?" Amber hoped for a moment she could distract him with a check and get him out of the cabin.

Warren acted like he had not heard her. "Working for you was supposed to be my break into the big league of high finance. But then, you had to go and ruin it for me.

"In high school and college, I was a geek. No one even noticed me. I was a minuscule speck of the paint on the walls. Guidance counselors and teachers were useless pieces of crap. I was a number on their roster. Their only concern was that I passed the required classes to graduate on schedule. They were clueless about how smart I was. They did not care about me. They taught me that adult wisdom was about as shallow as a mud puddle in the desert.

"At parties, I had to invent crazy stories about family vacations to the Amazon or the Pacific Rim, or I would stand unnoticed in the corner."

"Warren, that was a long time ago. I didn't go to school with you. Why now, why me?"

"Did I ever tell you about my mother when I worked for you? I hid from that woman the whole time I was growing up. Do you have any idea what it is like to have your own mother hate you? I never did anything right in her eyes. I used to think my old man might step in and help keep her off my back. But he complained as much as she did.

"I think I gave up caring what anybody thought about me in kindergarten. Why even try to please the world? In high school, I asked a few girls out. They said no. I quit asking. Jobs did not work out. Roommates took me to court. It's always been me against everybody else."

"Warren, I still don't get it. I'm sorry life hasn't been easy, but these struggles are behind you now. Let me go, and we both walk away from this with a few shattered nerves."

"Have you heard a word I said? Your time to dominate me and humiliate me is over. You're no better than the teacher in ninth grade who asked me if I wanted to help her do some yard work after school. I trusted her. I thought we were special to each other. I would have walked through fire for her. I even believed her when she told me I was handsome. Me, with this reddish-brown hair and these small gray eyes. Then a few months later, I overheard this woman come on to a real loser at school and say that he was special and had lots to be proud of. It was all the same stuff she had told me. Then she asked the runt to help her in the yard. I never felt so foolish in my life. I hope she rots in hell just like you're going to do.

"I don't think I smiled again until I found my June Bug. My love agrees with me. She understands how bad life has been for me. As soon as I'm done here, life will be flawless."

Warren rambled down one rabbit trail after another. Amber withheld comment, and he finally shut down and sat in silence. Amber felt his stare and looked him in the eye.

Amber attempted diplomacy. "Warren, there must be way more to this than what you have told me. None of it is making sense to me."

Warren stood and resumed pacing. "Let me help you connect some of the dots. If you remember, I worked a while with Melanie. You remember Melanie? I think she was one of your favorite employees," Warren taunted. "She and I didn't hit it off at first. She was aloof and condescending, but then, we recognized what we had in common. You, Amber, bringing you down was a goal we shared."

"You and Melanie? I don't believe it. You two would be the most unlikely pair."

She studied Warren's face and wondered how he could look relaxed and happy. His delight in Amber's present plight was apparent.

"Strange as it seems, it's true, but you got rid of her before we had time to conceive much of a plan. However, we weren't a pair in any sense of the word. We were partners in a scheme. A partnership can be based on innumerable facets. It would have been more fun and effective if we could have tormented you in the workplace. We met during happy hour at Izzi's and hatched a conspiracy. See how sophisticated and professional that all sounds."

Izzi's, a bar and grill one block from the office, was the popular destination of the majority of people leaving work on Friday afternoon. Amber had heard many tales about the good times at Izzi's, and Melanie had bragged about being out of commission on Saturdays because of Friday nights at Izzi's. Picturing it as part of Melanie's routine was easy; picturing Warren there took more imagination.

"Oh, I don't suppose you ever stepped foot in Izzi's. It was probably a little too earthy for you, too many common folks. What kind of swanky joint did you patronize on weekends, Amber?" Warren asked as his face flushed. "Knocking back a few beers and commiserating was one of the biggest highlights of my week. Meeting by meeting with Melanie made me realize how miserable my working conditions were. The lightbulb finally switched on when you received your last promotion. I should've backfilled you. I was right there under your nose. I should have been promoted into your old position. That's what I was working toward. I deserved to be your replacement. But we both know that didn't happen. You actually had the audacity to hire a headhunter to find an applicant. You never intended to open the doors into management for me."

Warren was half right. Amber had made an obligatory weak endorsement of Warren—rationalizing that a demanding position might be the ticket to his success. She had debated the proper course of action and in the end, knew she would have been a fool to take the risk of promoting him. Warren had not inquired about whether or not he was being considered and had not expressed any open interest in her position. He must have assumed he was. How presumptuous of him. His behavior and lack of performance would not open any doors for him. He was sharp enough to know that. He had become a jerk impressing no one, not his coworkers, and especially, not management.

Amber had hired him as someone with management potential, and he had started out showing promise. Out of the blue, he had gone squirrelly, and getting him back on track had been beyond her. The final decision had been Steven Kern's, and he had decided it necessary to go outside the company to find a qualified person.

Convincing Warren of this fact was not likely to happen at this point. Defending her actions would come off as lame excuses.

Amber's mind searched for a solution. Her memory bank was still empty. She had never been in this situation, or one remotely similar. She had no training. She would have to figure this out as she went.

"Like all the others, you were never satisfied, Amber. When you hired me, I truly believed my time had arrived. You were all peaches and cream at first. You helped me. Every now and then, you even praised me. It was almost an out-of-body experience. Then, like being backhanded by an angel, you turned on me.

"Pick, pick, pick. I could not do anything right. Want to know why I lost my focus? You. I lived for lunch and the phone calls with my love. Every minute in that place was a minute too long," Warren explained.

Amber could not believe what she was hearing and wanted to ask, "Did you honestly believe that it was wrong to expect someone to show up for work on time, to only take an hour for lunch and to keep personal calls to a minimum?"

"I know Steven Kern would have recognized my potential if you had not done everything in your power to isolate me. You wouldn't even let me make an appointment to talk with him. Remember telling me that's the way the corporate world operates, Amber?"

"It had nothing to do with you personally," Amber tried to explain. "I got all my directives from Mr. Kern. You were supposed to get all your directives from me. He was busy with his own direct reports."

"You held me back, and Kern was your puppet."

Warren and Melanie; their names kept repeating in Amber's head. Never in her wildest dream would she have put them together, not even in the same room. Warren was no match for Melanie's divisive antics. Finally, an "Aha" moment for Amber, and one piece of the puzzle fell into place. Melanie's devilish influence had precipitated the change in Warren's behavior and attitude at work. In all probability, Warren could have been successful if Melanie had not messed with him. She had been the instigator of this sick plot. The realization of Melanie's complete lack of scruples made Amber sad. Melanie might as well have been a vampire draining all his blood. She cared not for Warren, cared not that she was stifling his career. She had him under her manipulative spell—poor, helpless Warren. Her specialty was disintegrating the aspirations of her victims. Warren's future had been sucked out of him, and he was the clueless one.

Amber ignored the pain of her aching arms and plowed into the facts. "I had no idea you and Melanie were an item. That kind of news usually floods through the office."

"Oh, we weren't an item. Pushy broads aren't my type. Well, I take that back. There is a certain appeal to an assertive woman. You were what we had in common. You were the object of every conversation we had and, believe me, the reason for every meeting. But you held the upper hand. We ran into dead end after dead end. The most impact we had during all those months was stalking you and whistling an obnoxious tune. We were getting bored when Steven Kern trumped us, forced us to raise the stakes. Once you had lost your job, the game changed. Leaving your secure condo and staying in a remote area with an old man and a dog gave us the advantage. We decided to turn our harassment up a notch or two. Melanie was quite creative with the notes, don't you think?" Amber watched Warren's face lose its expression. He reminded her of a sad little boy who was unsure of what to do next. He stood motionless, and Amber thought he might cry. She waited for his next move.

"I could've walked away, got on with my life, because there is more to my world, a part I'm not going to share with you," Warren said.

"I thought you and my replacement had a good working relationship."

Warren walked to the porch window and looked out. When he spoke, his tone was melancholy. "When you move on, you don't look back, do you, Amber? If you'd paid attention, you would've known that bozo was impossible. He dismissed me from the get-go. It would have only been a matter of time before he gave me the boot."

"You left because you got a better job. You chose to leave and seemed excited about your new job in management, a department head, if I remember right."

"True, I resigned because I had landed another job, but I kind of overstated the facts. Department head was a stretch. I had two people reporting to me, whose jobs have since been eliminated. A machine now does their work."

"Oh, I had no idea," she said. She would have no way of knowing. She never had time for office gossip, and she had no legitimate reason to stay in touch with Warren. The idea that he thought she was supposed to be his personal savior at first angered her. Then, she realized she had lacked sensitivity for his personal shortcomings—had tried to deal with him on a business level, not an emotional level. Managing the department had not left her with much time to take care of people.

Amber analyzed Warren's statements and realized he had wanted her to be his friend. She had been his boss not his pal or psychologist. She had no inkling he expected so much of her. She had gone out of her way to mentor him, to help him along in his job. True, she had not wanted to get involved in his personal life. She asked, "How did that affect your job?"

"Oh, I've been moved from one department to another. They find grunt work for me and often send me on errands. I can be gone for hours, and no one notices. I'm a far cry from management. I put in my hours to get my paycheck—end of story. There is no upward mobility for me."

"Look at other companies, Warren. Find your niche. You don't have to settle." Amber knew her advice was too late to help Warren in his career. Rebuilding it would require starting at the bottom again and working his way up the ladder. A complete career change would be required at this point. She was not making any progress. She needed to focus on getting him to release her.

"Great advice coming from a boss who held me back. You're the reason I didn't get the promotion. You sabotaged me, and I've been backsliding ever since. There is no turning back now. Both our fates are sealed."

Amber decided it time to change the subject. "What happened with Melanie? Did you kill her?"

"Melanie had become obsessed. I think she flipped out. You know how difficult she could be. I had decided I didn't need her any more. You know how two's company and three's a crowd? When I told her, she went berserk, yelling and pounding on me. We had come to Westcliffe together and were just down the road a few miles. I had to shut her up. She was out of control. It wasn't part of the plan. It just happened. Wasn't it clever of me to put her body in the old man's yard? It was close to you, but not too close."

The irony of this flashed through Amber's mind. Westcliffe was not as melodramatic as she had thought. Vera was right. Amber had brought the drama with her. Amber pressed, "Who is this third party?"

Warren laughed. "That's my secret, and I'll never tell."

"Why did you ditch Melanie's car in the brush?" Amber grasped at any thread that might strike a chord with him.

"Well, I couldn't be seen driving it and had to get rid of it." Warren sounded proud of his accomplishment. "I've already told you how much I hate these mountain roads. I insisted that she drive that day, which, in hindsight, complicated the ordeal. It turned out to be one time when having my own wheels would have been easier. I don't like to be stranded."

Amber wanted to point out he should have been thorough enough to remove the registration. Instead, she asked, "How did you get back to Denver?"

"Oh, Amber, you're still trying to keep a step ahead of me. Guess what? I'm not going to tell." Warren laughed. "I see the wheels in your head turning. You won't figure this one out."

Amber knew he was right. Someone drove him back to Denver, and she was clueless as to who that might be. What really bothered her was whether the third party was from Denver or Westcliffe.

"Did Melanie know you had a gun?" Amber asked.

"Of course not. Melanie didn't want to put you out of your misery. She had an affinity for watching people suffer and mostly intended to harass you indefinitely."

"I still don't understand why you killed Brutus."

"Once you commit murder, Amber, there is no turning back. I had to continue. I no longer had a plan. I just let things play out. The dog was a nuisance. I decided to take him for a ride. My original plan was to keep him for a few days to drive you nuts. He just was too much to handle.

"Oh, and while we're talking shop, I had the honor of being called by Mr. Steven Kern himself. Seems he was snooping around the office about Melanie and someone informed him that the two of us were often seen at Izzi's. Get this, Amber. Kern and I actually met there. He bought me a drink, and I fed him a load of crap about you. I told you had gone off the deep end and were living here with an old man in a shack. I described how you had really let yourself go and told him you drank yourself silly every day."

Amber gasped. "How could you lie like that?"

"Once I got started, it was easy. I simply embellished everything I knew about your situation and spun it in a negative way."

"I can't believe Steven believed such untruths."

"Oh, he bought into every word. He was beyond shocked by the time our meeting was over."

Steven and Amber were well acquainted on a business level, but their relationship had been limited to the office. He had never asked, nor had she shared much about her life. Amber chewed on the thought. Steven should have been able to judge her by the daily behavior she exhibited. Yet he would have no reason to doubt Warren.

That explained why Steven never returned her call. He had investigated to a point and then was swayed to be wary of getting involved. Amber surmised he wanted to put as much distance between himself and her as possible. She fumed that he did not at least call her and ask a few probing questions.

"I offered him a deal from the get-go. I had information he wanted, and he could help my career. But he babbled on about a hiring freeze and nothing he could do for anyone. He really expected me to believe that. The price he paid for brushing me off was receiving inaccurate details about you. I think that it was a fair swap, don't you?"

"You're despicable!"

"Everyone is despicable, Amber. Think about it."

Joe, stooped and disheveled, appeared at the sunporch door and tried to open it. He looked in and let out a "hey!" when he saw Amber tied up in a kitchen chair. He shuffled out of view. Amber had watched for activity at Blake's during her lengthy interlude with Warren. She had tried not to let her disappointment show at no sign of Blake. Joe's truck had crawled out of Blake's lane minutes ago. She had kept a watchful eye but had not seen any other activity at Blake's. Her mind spun with questions. *Had Blake been home? Why weren't Ryan and Gavin coming to her rescue?*

"I didn't think the old man would be a problem, but I guess I'd better let him in before he runs off to squeal," Warren said as he headed for the sunporch door.

"Just ignore him," Amber pleaded. "He'll go away. He has dementia and won't remember what he saw by the time he gets home."

"Can't take that chance." Warren sounded like a professional thug.

Amber begged, "Please, he doesn't even have a telephone."
Warren unlocked the sunporch door and opened it wide.

"Run, Joe. Joe, run. Joe, run as fast as you can. He's going to hurt you. Go hide, Joe." Amber shouted over and over again—hoping her words would register in Joe's fragile mind.

"Shut up," Warren snapped.

With renewed strength, she struggled in her chair to free herself and watched as Warren stepped through the porch door and took aim with his pistol. Amber inhaled a deep breath, and in that split second, her eardrums exploded. She snapped her eyes shut and heard a thud. She was unable to determine if something hit the deck or the side of the house. She let out a primal scream that echoed through the serene valley.

Warren wore a creepy smile as he stepped back into the kitchen. "My luck is changing. Everything happens in threes. I didn't plan it this way. You were my only intention. The dog and old man are bonuses and complete the trilogy.

Amber's mind was on fire, and she needed to know if Joe was mortally wounded. She rationalized that Joe was a tough old geezer, and Warren could not be a good shot. Joe would be okay. She opened her mouth to correct Warren. If he killed her, she would be his fourth victim. She stopped. To bring him back to reality, she would need every weapon in her arsenal. Her mind raced, and she could feel her heartbeat in her throbbing ears. She couldn't let her life end this way? She had to talk some sense into Warren. Amber felt the blood rush to her face. The first words out of her mouth came from her heart, not her mind.

"You monster. You're evil. You must be the devil himself. How could you hurt an old man? Have you no compassion? There is no need to hurt anyone besides me. Don't bring anyone else into this mess!"

"Mess, mess," Warren echoed. "The word leaves a foul taste in my mouth. You're not helping, Amber. I'm tired of being yelled at. People who yell at me don't fare well. Why don't you just shut up?"

Amber kept her eyes on his right hand, which held the gun. His left came up and backhanded her across the face. Her head snapped to the side. Her lip pulsated and smarted. Her tongue found a split and licked the wound. She went silent, but her mind stepped into high gear. Warren had met her anger with anger. She would try reasoning with him one more time.

"Warren, you have always seemed like a sensible, intelligent young man. I'm afraid I don't have all the facts. I don't see the total picture. You're right. I'm not as smart as you. Tell me what I'm missing."

Warren's face relaxed a bit as he stared out the sunporch windows. His deranged mind momentarily overpowered by the magnificent grandeur of the mountain range. Amber saw a shadow move across the kitchen window. She took another quick look. The figure appeared again. She did not want Warren to follow her gaze, so she dropped her vision to the floor. Warren noticed the movement in the window as well.

"Looks like you have more company. Why's your cabin Grand Central Station today? You've invited too many people to this party Amber. Okay, change of plans. You and I are going for a ride. I've never ridden in a Jaguar before, but my time has come. I'm going to drive one." Warren fumbled with the leather lace and untied Amber. He grabbed the keys off the counter and said, "How convenient of you, Amber, to always leave your keys in the same spot."

Amber's arms were useless as they hung by her sides. Her only weapon remained her voice. "Warren, I know we can work this out. You've done nothing wrong. You've a good explanation that the authorities will understand. Let's talk to the sheriff. He's a friend of mine. I know he can help you. If you run, you aren't giving yourself a chance. You're selling yourself short, Warren." She might as well have been talking to outer space.

He pushed the gun into her back, and grabbed her arm with his slimy other hand. "Just walk to your car. You know by now that I can pull this trigger on a whim." Warren opened the front door, and they walked onto the porch, the porch where Amber would never see Brutus again—the porch she might never see again. One little bird flew away, and then the world seemed empty of life. Amber's hope of finding a yard full of lawmen with guns drawn instantly evaporated from her imagined plan. Warren pushed her forward, and she heard a soft moan. She started to bolt toward the end of the porch where Joe lay on his side. Warren jerked her back, and she landed hard on the porch floor. Joe's long arm reached in her direction. She tried to crawl to him, but Warren pulled her to her feet. More than anything else in the world, she wanted to go to Joe, get help for him, but her strength was no match against a delusional fiend. "Joe, Joe," she screamed in a foreign voice. Her emotions exploded and raced to every muscle her body. If Warren didn't have a gun, she'd rip his head off with her bare hands. Since that was not the case, her burst of anger sprang forth as hysterical cries. Warren dragged her off the porch and shoved her into the passenger seat of the Jag.

He kept his gun trained on her as he went around the front of the car and got in on the driver's side.

Warren started the engine, threw the gearshift into reverse, and cranked the steering wheel as sharp as it would go. The car spun 180 degrees and barreled out the lane.

SIXTEEN

Warren's forehead oozed perspiration, and he inhaled short quick breaths. "I hate these mountain roads."

As if reassuring a frightened child, Amber tried to provide comfort. "Warren, you're hyperventilating. Please slow down and take a deep breath. I'm so sorry. There's a huge misunderstanding. None of this is your fault. We can work it out. Please slow down. It takes practice to handle a powerful high-performance car. Even though I have driven this car many miles, I do not have the skills for high speed. At minimum, you need both hands on the wheel. I know that sounds really basic, but you can't drive with one hand."

Amber knew of no other way to try and get the gun from Warren. The car fishtailed around a bend and twirled into a complete spinout. Warren man-handled the Jag back into the ruts of the old road. The reflection of flashing red in the side-view mirror caught Amber's attention before the sound of a siren reached her. The chase was on. Warren pushed the gas pedal to the floor.

Amber's thinking kicked into high gear, racing to get ahead of the speeding car. An Eleanor Roosevelt quote dropped into Amber's mind: "A woman is like a tea bag—you never know how strong she is until she gets into hot water." Her situation had escalated from warm to hot when she had found Warren on the sunporch. The danger had gone from hot to boiling once the Jag had been fired up. The ability to think under pressure was how Amber navigated the corporate world. She knew she had to take action.

Warren spun off onto a side road from yesteryears. It was more appropriate for horseback riding or four-wheeling than vehicles. It was the same route she and Ryan had trotted along a few weeks ago.

The road snaked through forested areas and small open valleys. Ryan had said it was the back way to another small mountain town, the name of which escaped her. She scrambled to remember any landmarks she had seen. She had been so focused on remaining upright on Sally she had not noticed anything out of the ordinary, just typical mountain landscape. All she could picture was the imminent devastation that would occur when Warren wrecked the Jag. It would be the end of an intricately woven web of deceit spun by a couple of maniacs and would leave a messy carnage.

Then the image of a low washed-out area floated through her mind's eye. Piece by piece, a picture emerged. Along the trail, there had been a small burned area from a forest fire started by lightning. Ryan had explained that last summer there had been a record number of forest fires caused from many years of drought conditions. This particular fire had been a nit, easily extinguished with only a few acres torched. She scanned the countryside for the first sign of blackened trees. She searched from one side of the road to the other. The intermittent reflection of flashing lights in her side mirror provided some consolation. She still could not envision a rescue, but at least Ryan would be there when the end came.

In the distance, she saw the color of the pines begin to change, fading from fir green to variegated brownish-green. The speeding car was fast approaching the blackened landscape where the charred trunks stood.

"Warren, there is a section of the road up ahead, just at the bottom of this ridge, where the road has been washed away. If you go this fast, you'll tear the bottom out of this car. You must slow down to a crawl to cross there. It's very tricky. You'll need both hands on the steering wheel and intense concentration on the road to maneuver the car through that area. Going too fast will make it impossible for you. Please listen to me." Amber looked at Warren. "Please, Warren."

Warren dropped the gun into his lap and locked both hands on the wheel. The car wove all over the road. Amber placed her right hand on the door handle.

"There, there, you see it just ahead, Warren? Slow down to cross it. You can't get across the washout speeding like this. The others won't know it's here. It will disable their cars." In a steady and soothing voice, she kept warning him about the gully and how to handle the car. Warren kept his eyes straight ahead. Within twenty yards of the washout, he hit the brakes. The car lurched from side to side, and the rear end swung into the ditch. He wrestled the steering wheel with all his might. Amber braced herself against the door. The rear end of the Jag climbed back up onto the road as the front end entered the basin. The undercarriage hit hard, and the car bounced.

Before Warren could hit the accelerator, Amber snapped the door handle, pushed the door open, and leaned as far out of the car as possible. Using her legs as a springboard, she jumped out of the car and rolled in the dry dirt of the washout. The pain was instant and intense, but she willed her eyes to follow the car. Down the trail, the car sped like it was in a race for its life. The passenger door had flapped shut, and her dream car looked like a shimmering bullet streaking along the countryside.

Warren took the next hairpin curve, which came back toward Amber at full speed. The car left the road and flew through the air as if suspended by invisible cables from the heavens. It happened in the blink of an eye, but the scene played out in slow motion for Amber. She saw the car roll over before coming to rest at the bottom of a ravine, upside down like a dead animal. Through the fog of dust that lifted from the ground, she could make out the blackness of the tires as they continued to whirl at a high speed. The thunder of crushing metal and the explosion of gas roared back at her. Amber's world went black.

Amber heard voices. Someone called her name, or maybe two people were calling her name. She opened her eyes, blinking numerous times to bring the forms into focus. One concerned face of youth and the other of maturity stared back at her.

"Are you all right?" one of them asked.

"Well, I'm here, and my Jag is over there in that wall of black smoke and thick dust. My lower leg feels like it encountered an ax murder, and I'm going to scream with pain any minute. But the good news is I didn't see a white light beckoning me or hear my name being called." Suddenly, she sat erect. "Joe, we must help Joe."

Ryan and Blake looked at each other and nodded in agreement. "Joe's in a better place," Blake offered.

Amber retreated into a mute world, just as Joe would have done. She heard Ryan call for an ambulance and yelled at him. "I don't need an ambulance. Could someone drive me to the nearest ER?"

Blake and Ryan turned their backs to her and exchanged words. When they faced Amber, Ryan said, "Okay, here's the plan." The wail of another siren resounded around them. Before Ryan could continue, a second sheriff's vehicle and its siren slammed to a stop. "I'll take you and Blake back to his house, and he will drive you to Cañon City. Sheriff Rivers and I have some work to do."

Amber stole one look at Gavin River's handsome face before shutting her eyes. Mind over pain was the task at hand.

She sat in the passenger seat of Blake's immaculate truck with a bed pillow propped against the window to rest her head. They went the thirty-mile distance without speaking. After completing her paperwork, Amber waited her turn. "Blake, if there is something else you want to do in Cañon City, you don't have to stay with me. It looks like it could be a while before I even get taken into a room. And I know I'll need an X-ray. Any kind of test or procedure can really draw the ordeal out."

Blake shrugged his shoulders. "I can't think of anything. I don't do much business here."

Amber sat quietly and observed the comings and goings. No one ever seems to be in a hurry in the emergency room. Who knows how many different rooms she might visit and how many different medical personnel would perform some small part of her treatment. Amber was glad a mirror was nowhere in sight. She felt pale and dusty. If she had known she would have to wait so long, she would have washed her hands and face and combed her hair before leaving with Blake.

She looked at Blake and said, "I know you don't have a very good opinion of me, Blake. You were right. I didn't know much about how things are done around here. I came with my big city attitudes and haven't tried very hard to fit into the local culture. My closed mind deprived me of the opportunity to really enjoy the Western lifestyle. And I'm really sorry about Brutus. You had a right to not like him."

"It wasn't that I didn't like him. He was just a dumb animal. I very much hold his owners responsible. They were the problem."

"Did you have trouble with the Grants?" she asked.

"Oh, all the time. They just didn't get it. I don't know how many times I talked to them about Brutus, but they gave me blank stares. Sometimes, months went by without incident. The whole thing was unpredictable. You came after weeks of problems and confrontations. I had reached my wit's end and started taking shots at Brutus to get their attention."

"I'm disappointed in them. They never mentioned anything to me. A heads-up would have been helpful. Neither Vera nor Ryan had any knowledge of a problem. That really surprises me."

"Well, the Grants had no defense and knew it. People around here would not have shown them any sympathy. It's the law of the land with long traditional roots." Blake leaned forward and propped his elbows on his knees.

"That's understandable," Amber said. "You've had some real tragedies in your life. I'm sorry about your wife. It must have been hard to raise a child by yourself, not to mention lonely."

"Yeah, things happen. In a small community like this, it is hard to start over, hard to find something new to keep your mind occupied. I do the same things everyday and see the same people all the time. You don't feel like venturing too far when you don't have a companion to share new experiences with."

"Life is unfair sometimes. I really hope BJ will gain a better understanding of who he is—find his true north. Whether that is being a rancher or not is for him to decide. You want him to be happy."

"Yes, I would give my life for him. I tried not to let him go because he is all I have. I don't know what will happen to the ranch if he doesn't want it."

"There are lots of options. If he doesn't want to work it, he could rent it to someone. Your first concern should be reestablishing a relationship with him. After that, I'm sure the two of you can figure out a satisfactory plan to preserve the ranch for posterity."

Amber studied Blake's face. She decided the look she had interpreted as mad actually was a look of loneliness, and it veiled his rugged, chiseled features. She had missed the obvious. Blake was as lonely as Joe. They had lived in contrasting worlds but shared a strong common bond. A leitmotif that ran rampant in her life as well.

"Tell me about your place. Do you do all the work yourself, or do you have hired hands? I know nothing about the operation of a ranch," Amber admitted.

Blake walked Amber through the seasons, explaining all that must be done at different times of year. The more he talked, the more relaxed he became, and Amber hung on his every word.

"Calves are born in early spring, and typically, we get hit with a few snowstorms. We must go out and find the newborns and bring them into shelter. I have a 'hot box' in the barn that has a heating element in it to keep them warm. Every year, a few die because we can't find them in time. Later in spring, we spend a number of days branding the yearlings. During summer, the herds graze in the higher mountain pastures. In fall, we sell and ship some out. And before winter, we drive the herds to lower pastures where we can deliver feed to them by truck. That's pretty much the cycle with cattle." Blake finished his summary just as an ER attendant called Amber's name.

While Amber's leg was being set, Blake ate in the cafeteria and bought a sandwich to go for Amber. On the way out of the hospital, they stopped at the pharmacy to fill her prescription for painkillers. The doctor had given her a shot of morphine, and exhaustion was setting in. She dozed on the ride to the cabin. Once inside, Blake helped her into the living room where she said she would sleep on the sofa. He brought her a pillow and blanket, and she took one of her pain pills.

"Thanks for helping me, Blake. Even though the circumstances were a little weird, I enjoyed our time together."

"Is there anything else you need?"

"No, thanks. I'm good. I'm glad this whole nightmare is over." Her eyes drifted to the fireplace where she expected to see her problem pet stretched out. The place would never be the same without Brutus. Amber cried silent tears. She buried her head in the pillow as the huge vacuum in her heart opened up to a new kind of pain. She finally succumbed to slumber.

SEVENTEEN

A familiar voice whispered in her ear: "Amber, take these painkillers. You'll rest better." She felt pressure on her shoulder, and the voice came again. Sleep called her back, and she faded until something annoying blocked the pathway to rest and then released her. Before she entered a state of oblivion something called her back again. The muffled groans of a struggle, of pushing, shoving, and kicking tickled her consciousness. She forced the sounds out of her head, but they returned. In response to their amplification, she opened her eyes and saw the silhouettes of two people tussling and punching.

Amber struggled with her awareness. The scene seemed real, but it also seemed like a dream. It bounced back and forth in her head between real and unreal. She wished it away. She wanted to sleep, needed to sleep. The scuffling intensified, and she strained to focus on the two objects. She wondered why a man and a woman were wrestling. Her recognition of the man snapped her out of her fog. And even in the darkness of the room lighted only by the glow of the moon, she now recognized the woman.

"Blake, Olivia, what's going on?"

The action paused, and Olivia said, "I caught this man trying to give you painkillers."

"Blake?" Amber blinked like a beacon in a storm to bring her mind into focus.

"Don't listen to her," Blake commanded. "I don't know who she is or how she got in, but I woke up to find her trying to get pills down your throat."

Amber tried to think. Her head felt as if a big cotton ball had replaced her brain. Holding onto a thought was difficult. *Why are Blake and Olivia fighting? Why is Olivia here? Why is Blake here? Who was giving me pills?* She reached up and turned on the table lamp.

"Olivia, what are you doing here?" Amber asked.

"Go back to sleep, Amber. I'll take care of this guy. You told me how mean he is and how many times he tried to shoot your precious dog. Remember all the grief he caused you?"

"Oh, thank you, Olivia. What would I do without you?" Genuine appreciation came as easily as the accusation that followed. "What are you doing here, Blake?"

"When I brought you home from the ER, my intuition told me to stay with you," Blake said.

Olivia grabbed an odd-looking gun off the table, placed it squarely in Blake's thigh, and pulled the trigger. Blake fell to floor, rolling around like a new puppy.

"Take the rest of your painkillers, and we'll chat later," Olivia instructed.

The words had a familiar ring to them and echoed in Amber's ears. She took a deep breath, and her eyelids closed, taking her to a restful place. Her peace was pierced by the command: "Take your pills Amber."

Oh, yes. A female voice had delivered that order the first time. Layer by layer, Amber's thoughts began to connect with each other. Olivia was her trusted friend, and she was here to help. She would handle the problem. Amber's eyelids drifted shut. There was no need to worry.

Amber eyes popped open again like synchronized right and left jack-in-the-boxes. Amber could not figure out why Olivia was at the cabin.

"Olivia, what's going on? How'd you know I needed help?" Amber asked.

"I didn't expect the cowboy to be here dozing on the sunporch. He was snoring like a freight train, and I thought he was dead to the world. I tried to be quiet, but he woke up. His being here actually would have worked out well for me and would have provided the perfect scenario. I couldn't have written a better plot."

Amber stared at Olivia. The soft light of the lamp shined on the familiar facial features of her friend, but the personality of the person standing before her was that of a stranger.

"Olivia, what plot? What are you talking about?"

Olivia placed her hands on her hips, stood straight, and towered over Amber.

"The cowboy would have been the one placed at the scene of your overdose. I doubt the authorities would have looked any further. He could maintain his innocence and claim you did it on your own. The officials might buy that, or he would be convicted of your death. The two of you have a history of run-ins. He's known as an unfeeling, uncaring, pushy, miserable excuse of a man. Isn't that close to your own opinion, Amber? Either way, it wouldn't have been my problem."

"Why, Olivia, why are you trying to kill me?"

"You are so trusting and gullible, Amber. For as smart as you are, you are really slow to catch onto the obvious at times. At first, I thought you were great. I wanted to be like you. We were friends, and we had some good times. Those first few years we worked together were the best of my life, but then Kern fired me and promoted you."

"No, Steven didn't fire you," Amber said. "You decided to have an impact on humanity. I was proud of you. You were the only person I knew who could pull it off. It was so you."

Olivia rolled her eyes. "That was just a lie, just a cover up. I didn't want anyone to know he fired me."

"Why would he, and why didn't he say anything to me? He knew we were friends," Amber disputed the statement. She would have learned about something that big if it were true.

"Well, in simple terms, I embellished my resume a tad. I still think it's no big deal. Everyone does. Somehow, he found out. He must have been looking for a way to get rid of me because he was determined to consider it the biggest misrepresentation ever committed by mankind. He said if I resigned, he'd drop the matter."

Too bewildered to respond, Amber again sat up. As impossible as it seemed, Steven and Olivia had hidden the truth from her. *Fool* was the only word that came to her mind. She had been a Paul Bunyan–sized dope. "I can't believe I was such a patsy."

"There's more, Amber. You don't know the crème de la créme part of the farce yet. That day wasn't a total waste though. If you remember, my last day was Warren's first day."

"Warren? You don't know Warren," Amber said.

"It was a bit tricky keeping it from you, but he and I were an item from that day forward. Think about it. How much do you know about my life in the last couple of years? When was the last time we hung out together? When was the last time you were at my apartment?"

Amber added up the years. It had been a long time. It was explainable though because Amber had been spending her free time with Todd. Olivia had stopped inviting her. Their regular rent-movie nights were faded memories that belonged to someone else—a generation of herself from years ago.

"This was Warren and Melanie's conspiracy," Amber argued. "They both needed to get a life but found harassing me easier and more entertaining. Warren told me. He grew tired of the game, but he couldn't convince Melanie. He had to shut her up." As Amber verbalized Warren's explanation, his warning surfaced again. There was a part of his story he chose to keep to himself.

Enough pieces were in place for a picture to form for Amber. Olivia was the third party and Warren's trump card.

"Oh, I know all about Melanie. I was here with Warren a few times. Surprise! I didn't get as big of kick out of sneaking around as they did. I was taken back when Warren got rid of Melanie, literally, I mean. He never told me. I put two and two together when you told me the identity of the body. I wouldn't have missed her. Our paths never crossed. Warren was a go between. As long as he was having fun, why should I have cared about Melanie? I felt some uneasiness when he called me to come pick him up at the gas station in Westcliffe one day. He said Melanie went berserk when he told her he had changed game plans and didn't need her any more. He claimed she drove off without him. It sounded like something Melanie would do. Warren's obsession with you escalated after that. He should've finished you off on one of his nocturnal visits. You have no idea how many times he sat in this cabin or how often he watched you sleep. You would have never known. No one would've known. But he wanted you to know. There was no point to it if you didn't know in the end. Obviously, things didn't go as he had planned."

"I would've trusted you with my life, Olivia. I don't believe it." Amber's survival instincts kicked in. and she labored over what to do next. Keep her talking. *How long do the effects of a stun gun last?* "Olivia, this is not a very original plot. Are you making it up as you go along? Warren's not worth it, and you and Warren together? That's beyond belief."

"See, you're not as smart as you think you are."

"It has nothing to do with smart. I did think I was a better judge of character. We've been friends for years. I can understand Warren having a grudge against me, but you. I've never had any disagreements with you. We always got along."

"I was working for peanuts and had no chance of upward mobility. I had to take the only job I could get after Kern cut me off at the knees. I couldn't afford a condo, had to rent an apartment. You had everything."

"Olivia, you commendably gave up salary for the greater good. And your apartment is, is…nice." At the attempt to flatter Olivia, Amber remembered Olivia's apartment. Her memory of the building was that it was nondescript and kind of on the cheap side. Olivia did not decorate the space the way Amber would have, yet it seemed to reflect Olivia's personality. Olivia was drawn to contemporary, but rather than tasteful and arty, most of it was strange and lacked consistency from room to room. Each room was painted in a different bold color, and the furniture was eclectic. Amber had felt it matched Olivia's nature of nonconformity. Olivia could be impulsive, abrupt, and change her mind in a heartbeat. That was what Amber enjoyed most about Olivia. Amber viewed the apartment as perfect for Olivia.

"You always shunned opulence, put down rich people, made fun of their fancy houses and lifestyles. You didn't covet all that pretentiousness. How many times did you say you didn't need much to be happy? You were more interested in humanity than materialism," Amber reminded Olivia.

"I tried hard to convince myself that *less* is more. But it was a hard sell. When I met Warren, something changed in me. I didn't want to pretend any more. He and I were on the same wavelength. We both desired more. We both wanted what you have, all of it: the prestige, the power, the money, nice things. You don't even own anything that isn't extremely nice. Why should you have it all?"

"Olivia, I worked hard for everything I have. Nothing was handed to me. My priorities maybe were miscalculated at times, but…. I give up. You'll never understand. I'm still trying to wrap my head around your relationship with Warren. It's like a bad dream, almost laughable."

Olivia remained planted in one spot. Amber could not read her body language.

"Oh, Amber, this goes way beyond Warren. This is personal. You managed to take everything I wanted away from me. I didn't have anything against you except that you were Miss Perfect. That's what Warren and I called you, and you were Kern's pet. Everything always went your way—the golden-haired girl who could do no wrong. Warren was just going to torment you and scare you. He practiced and practiced picking locks. The porch door was one of the easier ones. I even came with him a couple of times to practice myself. It was all to be a summer of terror, laughs for us. But he got carried away and went too far. You see, Warren had issues and lots of baggage. Oh, by the way, your faithful watchdog was easy as well. At the sight of a bag of treats, he morphed into a pussycat."

"Olivia, I had no idea you harbored such resentment of me. The way you describe me isn't the way I see myself."

"You should take a better look."

"Why did you come tonight? Why tonight?"

"Warren didn't call me as usual. I tried calling him, but his phone was out of service. I knew something was wrong. You see. Warren depended on me. He needed me to stroke his ego. He couldn't go more than a few hours without talking to me."

"Olivia, you can leave now, and no one will care. Neither Blake nor I want you to be in trouble with the law. Go home. Don't throw your life away."

Olivia's response was swift: "I'm not, you see. Now, there's a new plot. I will kill you and your cowboy pal. No one will ever suspect me. This will be one unsolved mystery and will become the coldest case in the history of this little town."

The conversation with Olivia had bought some time, time for Amber to make sense of the soap opera, but Olivia now was talking about killing both her and Blake. Amber's mind spun as she thought *I'm as easily manipulated as Ryan. To think I judged him for allowing himself to be played. His was obvious, mine subtle, but I also am worldlier and should know better or should be sharp enough to have seen it—lied to by my best friend.*

The four d's—disappointed, disillusioned, disgusted, and disturbed—summed up the entire shocking day. She had gone out of her way to be nice and generous with both Olivia and Warren. She questioned why her efforts had gone unnoticed and certainly unappreciated, and how had she overlooked the envy and their need for power? And then the insight hit her with the brilliance of a solar flare. The biggest lie of all was the one she had been telling herself. *If it is a sin to lie to others, what is it to lie to myself?* She had believed in her happiness and had trusted it was shored up by a solid foundation. She had been sure that there was nothing more to life than what she had. Right now, she had nothing—not a dog, a friend, a boss, or a lover. She was going it alone.

"I drove to Westcliffe and went to the post office. I'm so glad you told me about Vera. She had all the details about a high-speed chase and some guy driving your Jag off the cliff. She said you'd be back from the ER tonight with a broken leg," Olivia said.

"I'm confused. I don't understand why you want me to die. I understand Warren's actions, but this is not you, Olivia."

"It's your fault Warren's dead. He is the only person I've ever loved. He can't have died in vain. You are responsible for me losing him and must pay a consequence. Warren was my puppet and..." Olivia stopped midsentence.

Amber's heart raced. She wanted Olivia to remain in her trance for as long as possible. Amber glanced at Blake, who was still not moving. Their eyes met, and an exchange of some understanding transpired.

Olivia held the stun gun and then fingered the trigger. "Sorry, I got lost in thought. It's over, Amber. I don't want to talk anymore. Take the pills, or I will stun gun you a dozen times. The end result will be the same."

Squirming around on the sofa, Amber acted as if she was going to refuse and intended to put up a fight. Suddenly, she took the glass of water in her right hand as if to lift it to her lips. In one quick motion, she threw the contents in Olivia's face. Blake sprung to a sitting position and tackled Olivia's legs from the side. She hit the floor hard and lost her grip on the stun gun. The impetus propelled it a short distance to the sofa. Amber wiggled to the edge of the sofa and stretched until the stun gun was in her possession. The fall had knocked the wind out of Olivia. She twisted her body and gasped for air. Blake handled her like a steer he had just roped. He rolled her onto her front and held her hands behind her back.

"This should be my last call to Ryan," Amber said more to herself than to Blake as she reached for the phone.

EIGHTEEN

Something inside Amber died that day. The last speck of childish innocence in her, that unquestionable trust in man, sucked its final breath. An overdue coming-of-age moment jettisoned her into the real world. It was a world where others lived, and she had visited on occasion. The consequences of not having her priorities straight had caught up with her, and her life had tumbled down around her. Her belief that hard work would make everything right was a falsehood. She felt empty. She had nothing more to give. The deceit hurt the most. Its pain threatened to last a lifetime. At first, tears would not come, and then they would not stop as the cleansing of her emotional clutter began.

Ryan had come in the night and taken Olivia away. Blake sat with Amber until morning when he had to attend to his ranch duties. Amber was alone. In the past, solitude was a state she enjoyed, one that fostered forward movement. The comfort in being alone with her own thoughts usually freed her. On this day, she longed for someone to console her and reassure her everything would work out in its own time.

She had escaped physical death twice in the last twenty-four hours. Wrapping her head around the facts was still a stretch. Her heart broke. The betrayal and scorn of the very people she had worked so hard to support and help boggled her mind. Pills masked the physical pain. Nothing from the pharmacy touched the pain of heartbreak. She tried to tell herself the painkillers were responsible for the roller-coaster plunge that her emotions were experiencing. After all her critical thinking and deep analysis, her conclusion was sobering. Her strongest attachment and healthiest relationship with living beings had been with Joe and Brutus. They wanted to be with her and expected nothing in return. The dichotomy of her recent affairs was that an old, old man and a mischievous dog had become dearer to her than anyone else in her life.

Amber ached for someone with whom to share her innermost feelings. She mentally inventoried those in her recent life who had reached out to her in some way, those who had shown an interest and not expected anything in return. Only two people made the short list. Ryan was first to come to her mind. He had a knack for being everywhere. That first unlikely meeting in the parking lot of the hardware store established their destiny of running into each other all over town. He had asked hundreds of questions about her lifestyle, probing for a visual of her world. He thought of others before himself to a fault and would never satisfy his own needs at the expense of another's. At earlier points in her life, his strong family ties would have suffocated her. Now, she found it *sweet*, an extremely unsophisticated word she seldom used. If she were feeling blue, she would want Ryan in her presence. He had a heart as big as a house, but his visions and goals were pea-sized. He was happy taking life a day at a time and had no itch to experience anything different. That lifestyle would be a stretch for Amber. She was more accustomed to take charge men with drive, even if they were headed in the wrong direction.

Blake had depth and wisdom but too much baggage. He needed a good friend, a diversion from the ranch, and time to reinvent himself apart from his heritage. He was nobody's fool. Yet, he had some stepping out to do before entering a serious relationship. Amber could envision spending hours talking to him. He had successfully used a boatload of life experiences and pain to his advantage. His strong character was well-rooted and solid. Amber had never met anyone who was as sure of himself as Blake. If she were shipwrecked, she would want him beside her.

She had no intention of being blue or shipwrecked. Amber had matters to attend, plans to make, and places to go.

She hobbled upstairs and painstakingly secured a plastic bag around her cast before stepping into the shower. As the water droplets tapped against her shoulders and neck, she closed her eyes and let the mist renew her pores. She thought of nothing and concentrated on the therapeutic massage that blessed her from the showerhead. Her mind was blank, and she lingered in that state until an inner voice told her the time had come. A new attitude radiated from her cleansed body as she stepped out of the shower stall. She styled her hair and selected her most colorful outfit. And someone different hobbled down the stairs. Beneath the exterior and all the way to her core, the conversion Amber had craved and pursued completed its transformation. *Thanks be to God!* she thought.

Amber mentally rehearsed what to say to the Grants. Other than being remorseful and honest, comforting them across the waters would be difficult. Anticipating that Ilene might fall apart caused Amber to question whether she could keep herself from breaking down. If Amber started to cry, she would need a few minutes to recover. She preferred to be viewed as composed rather than as a blubbering airhead. She mustered up all the emotional stamina she could each time she dialed the phone. After numerous tries at different times of the day, Amber was able to make the connection.

"Hello, Ilene. This is Amber Hanson. I'm so sorry to bother you but I—"

"Oh, Amber, we have had the most incredible time. It is evening here, and we are just on our way out the door to cruise down the Danube through Budapest. The history of this city—"

"Ilene, I'm sorry," Amber interrupted. "This isn't a social call. Please listen to me. I've some bad news about Brutus." Amber informed Ilene of Brutus's death. "I can't tell you how sorry I am. He was a really fun dog. The place is not the same without him." Amber's voice quivered as she choked back tears. "I'll gladly buy you another dog, if that will help. I apologize for giving you this information over the phone. It is a rather long story that I can tell you when you get home."

"Oh, that's okay, dear. We already heard about Brutus and Joe in fact."

"I'm terribly sorry about both of them. I know you'll miss Brutus."

"I'll make this brief because we need to get to the boat dock. It's true. We were attached to Brutus, but having been gone these months has lead us to reevaluate our lifestyle. We've decided we want to go as many places as possible in the next few years, and that requires us to sell our property in Westcliffe. So, in the end, we would've had to part with Brutus anyway. We aren't sure when we are returning to the States, but you can leave whenever you want. Just lock up and leave the key with Vera."

And that was that. "Brutus, good buddy, I didn't see that coming," Amber spoke to the heavens.

One more call to go. Amber stalled as long as she could before making her obligatory call to her mom. With as much perkiness as she could summon, she recapped the highlights of her summer. She played down the danger, spun the details to sound mundane, and hoped her mother would not go into a tailspin over the unbelievable drama surrounding each major event.

"I'm really sorry everything got so offtrack for you, Amber. I'm shocked. I can't believe this is real. You have been through so much. Would you like me to come get you or have you made other arrangements to get back to Denver?"

Relief leapt inside Amber. Her mother seemed unalarmed. Amber had slicked over the magnitude of the happenings. She had passed the first hurdle. "No, I haven't thought that far ahead. Actually, that would be nice and very helpful, Mom. Guess I'm kind of stranded. I really appreciate your thoughtfulness. Could you come in four days? I need to take care of a couple of things here."

Amber and her mom worked out the details. As she hung up the phone, she let out a deep sigh. The phone call had ended without her mom passing judgment. Amber had expected the standard comments: "I knew this would happen. Why don't you listen to me?" They had made it through the long conversation without a lecture, but it would come. Sooner or later, it would be delivered.

***

Three days later, Amber memorialized Joe in a simple service attended by Blake and Ryan. The glumness of customary funeral clothing seemed unfitting for the natural setting. Amber chose to wear a flowing aqua skirt and white silk blouse. The guys wore jeans and cowboy boots. Ryan's pale-blue shirt intensified the blue in his eyes, and Blake's burgundy shirt screamed masculinity. Amber stood back and took a long look at them.

"You both look dashing. If anyone else was coming, all eyes would be on you."

"You look pretty snazzy yourself," Ryan said.

Amber gave thanks that Joe's earthly struggles had ended and took comfort in the thought that he deserved to rest in peace. The grief and moroseness of Joe's passing was short-lived. The release from the events in his life that tortured him daily was a cause for celebration in itself. Amber hated the unnatural and unnecessary way Joe died. It horrified her that a mild-mannered man who probably had never raised his voice should die at the hands of violence. Her one consolation was the fact that his survival through another winter in his primitive cabin was unlikely.

Amber stood in the clearing surrounded by trees and reflected on her short time with Joe. The unfairness of being shortchanged in the longevity of their friendship could anger her, if she chose to let it. She preferred to concentrate on the blessings he had brought her and how she cherished the last days spent with him. She had made arrangements for a private service with a funeral home and buried him in style: decked out in a dark suit, white shirt, and red tie. She had given the mortuary two of Joe's favorite books to be placed in the coffin beside him. A spray of colorful wildflowers draped his bronze casket and completed the theme. Amber regretted that his birthday cake still sat on the counter untouched. She had wanted him to have that experience before leaving this world. She also realized, at his age, the celebration would have meant more to her than to him. That acknowledgement failed to stop the cake from taking on a symbolic meaning, a kind of unfinished business that Amber could not dismiss. The thought lingered heavy in her soul. She pushed the image of the stale cake out of her mind. She would deal with it in due time.

Amber spoke the eulogy and led the others in prayer. A gentle breeze hummed through the pines, and birds sang a melodic tone to one another, performing a rendition of the only music Joe would have known and appreciated. Her eyes misted. Though circumstances dictated the simple fanfare, no amount of extravaganza could have trumped the fact that Joe had a death certificate. There now was a record of his life—his name written in history.

The sun hung at the apex of a flawless sky. Amber watched two adolescent chipmunks play tag, scurrying on the ground, and swishing up and down rocks. She deemed them to be a portrayal of Joe and one of his siblings having fun, frolicking freely for a moment in time.

"This is the perfect place to leave Joe. I'm glad there was enough space for him beside Sarah. His family and this property were his world and all he ever knew. This is where he belongs," Amber said.

Blake concurred as if spoken more for himself than Joe. "A man belongs with his roots."

As they stepped out of woods onto the path to Joe's house, Amber was overcome by a yearning to go to her favorite outcropping and sit in her special spot one last time. She froze in her tracks.

"What's wrong? Do you need help walking?" Ryan asked.

"No, I'm feeling called to Redemption Ridge," Amber answered as she swayed on her crutches.

"What?" Puzzlement was written on Ryan's face.

Amber explained, "For months, I have been trying to name my perch at the back of Joe's property where I meditated, prayed, thought, and basked in the beauty of the setting. Every day, I pondered over an appropriate designation. Hundreds of names went through my mind. Here, without thinking, it drops out of nowhere."

"Redemption Ridge," Blake repeated.

"Brutus and I spent hours there." Amber took a step. "I guess a certain amount of recovery and purification did happen there."

"Would you like us to help you get there?" Ryan asked.

"Heavens no. It would be impossible on crutches. You both are very physically fit, but I don't think you are capable of climbing a mountain, even a small one, with me on your back," Amber replied. "Thank you for the offer, but I can be satisfied with my memories." She turned in the direction of Joe's house.

The three strolled along the path. Walking on crutches took twice as long and Amber apologized. She offered for them to go ahead without her. Both Blake and Ryan said they had no reason to hurry and offered their assistance. Amber politely refused their chivalry and took every step on her own.

"Can you imagine how tangled up Brutus would have gotten in my crutches? I don't think I could have handled him and them. Guess you would have had to take him for a while, Blake," Amber teased and waited for Blake to protest.

To her surprise, he mumbled, "We would've worked something out."

"Walking this usual route without Brutus romping about seems odd, but strangely enough, it feels pleasant too, as if everything is in place," Amber shared and then resumed her trek.

When they neared Joe's house, Blake said, "Let's stop in Joe's cabin. There is something he wanted you to have."

"What? How would you know what Joe wanted?" Amber said. "Joe never talked to you. Joe didn't know he was going to die."

"I'll explain everything in a minute. Don't be so impatient," Blake answered.

"I'm sorry, Blake. I didn't mean to sound accusatory. I'm just taken by surprise."

"I know. If it doesn't make sense, you're going to pounce on it."

Amber sighed. "Let me try again. How thoughtful of him. I would cherish anything that had been Joe's."

Blake opened the front door of Joe's house as wide as it would go, and Amber shuffled through it. She breathed a number of quick breaths as a sense of alteration came over her. Without Joe present, the house took on its own air of departure. Amber hesitated in the main room, which looked ancient and tired. She saw nothing worth resurrecting. It had fulfilled its purpose, and its lifespan had come to an end. One more blizzard, and the walls would collapse around the meager contents. She was at peace with letting nature take its course. The happening would be apropos, not sad.

Amber followed the guys into Joe's makeshift library, where Blake picked up a folded piece of paper from the old desk and handed it to Amber.

She unfolded the paper and read silently the words written in the familiar perfect penmanship. "Wow, this can't be right," she gasped. "This is Joe's last will and testament, and he's leaving the Stoner ranch to me." Either she had overdone the physical exercise, or her emotions were giving her a buzz. She began to rock on her crutches. She needed to sit down. Blake placed a wooden chair next to her and took her crutches from her.

"How great is that?" Ryan beamed. "Now, you can become a resident of Westcliffe."

Ryan's timing was precise. His excitement counterbalanced Amber's concern for the impact of Joe's actions. Her inner voice advised her to enjoy Joe's generosity and loving gesture for the moment and worry about the consequences later.

"Joe's mental state wasn't stable enough for him to sign a legal document that would stand up in court. And, Blake, you signed as Joe's witness. I didn't think the two of you had ever been in the same room."

"Well, as unbelievable as it seems, Joe came to my house a couple of weeks ago and asked me to witness his signature. On that day, he was as lucid as you or me. He was insistent that I keep the document in my possession, said he had no safe place to keep it at his shack. He knew exactly what he was doing. No question about it. But I had doubts myself about the legality and called my lawyer. He did some research and says there is no one to contest the will. He sees no problem moving it through probate."

Blake's assurance alleviated her practical concerns, and she allowed her emotions to speak: "That is so special. I would have been happy with some of his books. I don't know what to say." Amber thought the well was empty, but a couple of tears managed to slide down her cheek. "Oh, Joe, what a sweetheart you were. And thank you, Blake, for being a trusted friend to him in the end."

"I debated on when to give you Joe's will. I decided that picking it up from his house would make it seem more like he was presenting it you," Blake explained.

Ryan browsed the contents of the crates, muttering a title every now and then. Blake sat on the edge of the old desk and explained, "There was a lot more to old Joe than I thought. He and I had a long visit that day. We had agreed to visit each other on occasion. I think we would have. We had a lot of common ground, and he was more educated than I had expected. He knew a lot of stuff."

"Yes, he was sharp for his age and background. There was so much he could have taught the world if he'd had the chance," Amber added.

Amber reached for her crutches. "Well, let's go have a nice lunch in remembrance of a truly remarkable man with an incredible life story."

They walked to the Grants' cabin where Amber served lunch on the sunporch. That morning, she had started barbecue beef in a Crock-Pot, made potato salad, and cut cantaloupe and watermelon into wedges. She also had managed to assemble her signature coconut cream pie before collapsing on the sofa from overdoing and to amass enough energy to proceed with a funeral.

Her nerves overran exhaustion, and she relaxed and luxuriated in the company of the deputy and rancher. Laughter resounded around the room, through the open windows and wafted into the mountain air. The unlikely trio reminisced about the events of Amber's tenure, the excitement as Ryan called it. Blake insisted it was a catastrophe, and Amber saw it as pure drama.

The mantel clock struck four, and Blake bounced to his feet. "I didn't realize it was so late. I must get home. Amber, I've been thinking about Joe's possessions. You're not going to have time to take care of them before you leave. Sometime in the next few weeks, I'll bring some boxes and my truck. I'll pack up everything and store the boxes at my place until you're ready to go through them."

"I can't let you do that. That's too much work. I can change clothes and go work on it right now. I haven't had time to think about it. I guess his cabin will be abandoned for months. And if it falls down, the books will be ruined. I care only about his books. None of the rest appears to have any value. The other stuff is too old and dilapidated for charity and too common to be sought after as antiques. The rest, I can deal with later." Amber rose and steadied herself as she reached for her crutches.

"No, you're in no shape to be packing boxes. Please let me do this for you. I'll only get the books."

"If you insist, I will let you do that, but just that. And one more thing, Blake, would you keep an eye on Joe's pickup? That's worth restoring and keeping in Joe's memory."

Amber thanked Blake again and hobbled to the front porch with him. "I will keep in touch with you, Blake. If you feel like taking a field trip some day, let me know. There are hundreds of places I could take you in Denver. Some of them, I think, you'd enjoy very much."

They exchanged an awkward congenial hug, and he jumped off the porch rather than use the steps to depart for the last time.

When Amber went back inside, Ryan had cleared the dirty dishes from the sunporch and was humming a tune as he opened the dishwasher.

"I can manage to load the dishwasher, Ryan. You've done the hard part. I know one thing for sure. I'm going to be tired of being a gimp by the time this cast comes off."

"Walking on crutches into a job interview might have its advantages," Ryan teased.

"What? Someone will take pity on me?" Amber asked.

"An icebreaker at least. Of course, you won't want to disclose the circumstances around the wild ride that led to your disability."

"That's going to be hard to explain even to someone who knows me." Amber bit her lip. "On a serious note, Ryan, I've been thinking. I know you'll balk at this, but could you encourage BJ to contact his dad? He doesn't have to come back to the ranch, but Blake needs him. I know you don't want to get in the middle, but someone must make BJ understand that loneliness is consuming Blake. He needs his son. BJ is all he has."

Ryan wiped his brow with the back of his hand. "I know. It all makes more sense to me now. I'll see what I can do."

"Thank you, Ryan. You're a true friend. I hope Meredith knows what a great guy she has."

"I tell her every chance I get!"

"While you're at it, could you introduce Blake to a nice suitable lady who could add some spice to his life?"

Ryan shook his head. "Now, that I'm staying out of. I'm sure I'd make a royal mess of that."

"Yeah, that is a big ask. I wouldn't know how to go about that either," Amber confessed. "And, Ryan, I hope you know that I tried very hard not to get involved with Rachel. I mean I enjoyed talking to her but encouraged her at every chance to talk to her parents or you. I didn't invite her to the cabin. She just showed up, but then I felt obligated to keep her safe. She would take advice only to a point and was determined to do things her way, pretty typical of someone her age, I'd say."

Ryan leaned against the counter and crossed his feet. "I know. She can be very difficult and unreasonable. Sounds like you made more inroads with her than I ever did."

"Don't take it personally. I'm sure she didn't care what I thought, which made it easier for her to talk to me. She cares what you and your parents think. Have you heard from her?"

"No, not a word," Ryan said.

"Well, we know she rode off with Jackson. That is some comfort. She is not out there alone," Amber said.

They both ran out of words at the same time and stood muted and motionless.

Amber's leg ached, and she shifted her weight. "Time for a painkiller."

"You look tired. I'm going so you can rest. It has been a long day. Thank you for lunch. Joe's burial was simple yet elegant. But I think that is how you do everything."

The room fell silent again. The dreaded moment of saying good-bye had come.

"Well, the next time I see you, you'll probably have exchanged your hiking boots for cowboy boots," Ryan spoke first.

"An urban cowgirl. I could replace the Jag with a souped up '52 Ford pickup. Nah, I think not."

They both tossed their heads back and laughed.

"I don't know when I'll be back. I'll send you a Christmas card. By then, I should have lots of updates to pass along," Amber promised.

"I'll give you a call because I don't do cards," Ryan said.

Both nodded. Amber leaned her crutches against the kitchen counter, and Ryan moved toward her. They embraced in a tight hug and released without looking at each other. Ryan went in the direction of the front door. Amber scooted to the kitchen sink and gulped down a painkiller. Her back was to the door when she heard it close. She made her way to the sofa where she collapsed and napped until the physical pain was gone.

NINETEEN

t times, Amber thought the night would never end. Finding a comfortable resting position with a cumbersome cast presented a challenge. She left her bed in the loft about midnight and went downstairs to sit in a recliner. She slipped into a deep sleep, and when she opened her eyes, sunlight filled the room. She worked her way to the kitchen to prepare a cup of tea.

As she reached for a cup from the cupboard, she noticed Joe's birthday cake on the counter. She stared at the piece of unfinished business. She had neglected to add it to her long list of tasks. She realized the time had come to make it a priority—time to toss it into the trash. She fingered the cake plate, massaging the rim as if her mind was on hold. Then her intuition set her in motion. With the resolve of marching off to war, she shut the cupboard door and hobbled upstairs. She threw on a pair of sweatpants and shirt and left her hair uncombed. She made her way back to the kitchen. She placed the cake in a bag with handles, took up her crutches, and headed outside. She was so intent on her assignment that the sights and sounds of the natural world lay beyond her awareness. For this last act of kindness, none of it mattered. Walking as fast as she could, she looked straight ahead as she maneuvered the familiar path. She motored on without turning her head to look at Joe's house and stopped when she had reached his gravesite.

The mortuary had completed the interment, and his spray of wildflowers swept over a mound of fresh dirt. At the head of the grave was a marble cross bearing his name and date of his death. She had paid a hefty fee to expedite the engraving and delivery of the tombstone. Having the marker in place brought closure.

She kneeled at the head of his grave, removed the cake from the bag, and placed it at the base of the cross. She pulled two blue columbines from the spray and pressed them into the cake. Her form became a statue, stiff and silent as she mentally spoke to Joe. When she stood, her heart was filled with satisfaction. It was time to tend to the preparations for leaving.

<hr />

Amber's mother drove into the yard about noon. She loaded Amber's belongings into the car and wandered around the cabin while Amber conducted a final walk-through. When she returned to the front porch, Amber was coming out of the house.

"The views are captivating. I had forgotten how beautiful the mountains are," her mother said. "It has been a long time since I have been in the mountains. Guess tourists do it; locals don't."

Amber closed and locked the door of the Grants' cabin for the last time and responded, "There's probably some truth to that, but it's more likely that anything at hand tends to be taken for granted. It's hard to be deliberate without a compelling reason."

As they slid into the car seats, Amber said, "After I lose this cast, maybe you and I can spend a weekend in some small mountain town."

"Maybe," her mother replied.

Amber did not look back as they drove out the driveway. She had her mother stop in front of Joe's so she could take a long look in an effort to etch every detail into her mind.

"If I weren't seeing this place in person, I wouldn't believe it. This place is a mess, a real eyesore. What are you going to do with it? I think you inherited a headache," her mother said.

Amber didn't respond. Through her own filters, she saw the scene as nostalgic and historic. It told the story of the life of a family, of real people, engaged in their own private battles. And then there was the property to the back that painted a contrasting picture. The first day Amber had encountered the junkyard and run-down buildings, she had been as appalled as her mother. Today, she found the scene heartwarming.

Amber sighed. "On the surface, it does wreak of slovenliness. It's what is underneath all the scrap that tells a story and melts your heart."

Amber kept the Hunter ranch in sight as long as possible. She thought she saw Blake standing in the front window, and her heart leapt. On second thought, it could have been a reflection on the glass, which was better in reality.

"There really isn't much going on around here," her mother said.

Amber answered, "It's deceiving."

The car skimmed along the countryside, and Amber stayed focused on the Sangre de Cristo Mountains. After passing Four Corners, Amber said, "I just need to zone out for a minute and be alone with my thoughts, Mom. Don't be alarmed by me not talking for a while."

Her mother took a hard look at her. "You often don't talk, Amber. I'm used to it."

"Yeah, you're right."

In Westcliffe, they made one last stop at the post office. Amber's mother kept the car motor idling while Amber dropped off the key to the Grants' cabin and her post office box key. For old times' sake, she checked her post office box. Her hand recoiled at the sight of another card. Her heart fell to her feet. *Don't panic,* she told herself.

Amber slipped the card into the back pocket of her pants before making eye contact with Vera, who was dressed in the same denim jumper as the first time Amber had met her.

Vera spoke first, "On your way back to the city?"

"Yes, there's nothing more to do here. I'm sure you know I'm to leave the Grants' key with you."

Vera put one hand on the counter and the other on her hip. "Who knows when, or if, those two characters will be back since their house already sold."

Amber took a step closer. "The cabin is sold? How's that possible?"

"As soon as Sheriff Rivers heard it was going on the market, he made the Grants an offer, and now, it's a done deal," the live local newscaster reported.

"Gavin?"

"He's an interesting fellow. He—"

Amber cut her off, "That's okay. I'm in a hurry. I don't need to know anything more about Gavin at this time."

Vera changed subjects without a pause. "I wonder what will happen with Joe's property."

Amber could feel her smile almost spreading from ear to ear. "Time will tell," she exclaimed as she turned and walked out of the post office.

All the loose ends fell into place, but what delighted Amber the most was that Blake and Ryan had treated her business confidentially. Westcliffe had not yet learned that she had become a property owner. She would get out of town before the word got out and tongues started to wag.

Amber unintentionally looked up and down the side streets for a glimpse of Ryan's beat-up truck or his sheriff's cruiser. The streets were empty, and she was glad. Good-byes had already been said. Closure had been made. The time had come for her to get on with her life. Main Street looked the same as on the day she waited in the café for the Grants, but she now knew that behind that quiet facade, real life abounded with all its joys, sorrows, and crazy behaviors of mankind.

"Setting aside all the problems you had this summer, how did you like Westcliffe?" Amber's mother asked.

"Um, all in all, I think it is a nice little town. I find it a bit confining. I can't see myself becoming a full-time resident, but I do think it'll be a great getaway, retreat place for me someday."

Amber shared another epiphany: "I had given up on trusting anyone, but I guess some men can be trusted. Blake and Ryan are both quite extraordinary. I don't know what I would have done without them."

"You know better than that. Put your trust in God. Sooner or later, people always let you down. It's human nature."

The sparse words stirred sadness in Amber; the reality of their truthfulness was undisputable. "Yes, I know Mom. You're right." She found it hard to believe she not only said the words—but also meant them.

Amber squirmed in her seat and wiggled the card out of her hip pocket. She studied the envelope and said, "This mail is addressed to me in Westcliffe. There is no post office box number or return address."

"That's impossible," her mother said. "Mail can't be delivered without a complete address."

"You'd be surprised at what can be done by the Westcliffe post office." Amber opened the envelope and took out a small piece of notepaper folded in half and read it silently.

Dear Amber,

This request will seem very immature and pushy of me, but I have nowhere else to turn. Jackson and I came to Wyoming as planned, but he is a different person here. We fight about everything, and I am miserable. I now know that our marriage is over. I see nothing worth saving. I don't know where to go or how to begin on my own. I am so, so sorry to ask you this. I know I have no right to ask, but I need a neutral place to land while I get myself sorted out. Can I stay with you for a while? I will be honest with you. I don't know how long my stay might be. I feel I must get away from all my family to totally be free to start over on my own.

I hope this letter finds you before you return to Denver. I haven't been in touch with anyone from Westcliffe since I left. I will understand if you say no, or even if you do not answer me.

It was signed Rachel with a phone number under her name.

Amber's eyes had misted, and a lump formed in her throat. The note had a heartfelt yet naïve tone. Rachel was straight-out asking for Amber's help, and Amber heard her plea. Yes, she would give Rachel whatever help she could. Whether the commitment was for one or two years, Amber would be supportive but would let Rachel make all her own decisions. She wouldn't make any of the same assumptions as she had with Olivia and Warren. Amber had a guest bedroom fit for a queen that had been used a few times. Rachel could claim it and change it to suit her own tastes, whatever they might be. Even though adopting a young adult was out of her league experience-wise, she would figure it out one day at a time. Sharing the condo was a new direction for Amber too, and she welcomed the challenge.

"Bad news?" her mother asked about the note.

"Well, yes and no. A friend I made in Westcliffe needs my help. I hope my help will be enough to make a difference."

"You've befriended many people before Amber and have helped them. I'm sure you'll do the same with this one."

"No, I don't want to help on the surface. I want to become connected and help at the core of the problem."

Amber's mom looked at Amber and smiled a tender smile that startled Amber. Amber jerked her head to the mountainside for a moment of reflection. When she turned back, her mom's eyes were on the windy road. Amber was mesmerized by her mom's profile. The lady was attractive with silver streaks in her dark shoulder-length hair. Character lines danced around her eyes. She had been working out at the YMCA with a group of ladies from church and looked trim for her age. For as long as Amber could remember, her mother had been neat and fussy about her appearance. Her wardrobe was inexpensive, much of it bought at discount stores, but her mother wore them with the same care and pride as she would a designer label. If she had to credit her mom with some influence, it would be a flare for tasteful fashion, even though Amber's clothes were expensive.

For the remainder of the drive, Amber composed a to-do list for when she arrived at her condo. First, she would call Rachel and have her come to Denver ASAP. If need be, Amber and her mother could drive to Wyoming and get her. Second, she would call Steven Kern to square the record with him and then write him out of her life. Third, she would go car shopping. As the list formulated in her mind, her spirits lifted. There was so much to do.

Amber was returning to Denver where she would find comfort in her beloved condo, but she now had a sense of the changes she had to make in her life to move forward. She was primed to take on a new job, something challenging but not all consuming, and to establish new friendships with real people who knew each other's flaws and weaknesses, hopes, and dreams. One junkyard issue from the past remained—*the question of what to do with her inheritance.* As with every other issue surrounding Joe, Amber knew the answer would come when she least expected it. And when it came, it would likely be some inconceivable, unimaginable feat set before her. She needed time to figure that one out.

Lots of time.

AFTERWORD

Westcliffe is a real place as are some of the aspects of living there. However, *Redemption Ridge* is a fictional tale. Some landmarks mentioned in the book exist. Others do not. Depiction of the geography and events, though based on facts, are not intended to be factual or accurate. Like the characters, they are solely the vision of the author.